The Cove

ALSO BY RON RASH

FICTION

Burning Bright

Serena

The World Made Straight

Saints at the River

One Foot in Eden

Chemistry and Other Stories

Casualties

The Night the New Jesus Fell to Earth

POETRY

Waking

Raising the Dead

Among the Believers

Eureka Mill

ecco
An Imprint of HarperCollins*Publishers*

The Cove

Ron Rash

This book is a work of fiction. References to real people, events, establishments, organizations, or locales are intended only to provide a sense of authenticity, and are used fictitiously. All other characters, and all incidents and dialogue, are drawn from the author's imagination and are not to be construed as real.

HarperCollins books may be purchased for educational, business, or sales promotional use. For information please write: Special Markets Department, HarperCollins Publishers, 10 East 53rd Street, New York, NY 10022.

Designed by Mary Austin Speaker

Library of Congress Cataloging-in-Publication Data has been applied for.

ISBN 978-0-06-180419-9

12 13 14 15 16 OV/RRD 10 9 8 7 6 5 4 3

For my sister, Kathy Rash Brewer

ACKNOWLEDGMENTS

Frank O. Braynard's *"World's Greatest Ship": The Story of the Leviathan, Volume 1* and Jacqueline Burgin Painter's *The German Invasion of Western North Carolina* were especially valuable sources in writing this novel, and are excellent reading for anyone interested in learning more about the *Vaterland* and the Hot Springs camp. The newspaper article in chapter 15 was published in the November 5, 1916, issue of the *New York Times.*

Grateful appreciation to Marly Rusoff, Mihai Radulescu, Lee Boudreaux, Abigail Holstein, Tina Monaco, Phil Moore, Bill Koon, George Frizzell, Kathleen Dickel, Tom Rash, Lea Kibler, Western Carolina University, Ann, James, and Caroline.

Her eyes were open, but she still beheld,
Now wide awake, the vision of her sleep:

JOHN KEATS, "THE EVE OF ST. AGNES"

The Cove

PROLOGUE

The truck's government tag always tipped them off before his Kansas accent could. After a decade of working for the TVA, he'd learned the best reception to hope for was a brooding fatalism. He had been cursed and spit at and refused a place to eat or sleep, his tires slashed and mirrors and windshields shattered. Knives and guns had been drawn, pitchforks and axes wielded.

But it had been different here. There was no one to evict and, once he explained where the lake would be, no more glares or sullen words. You can't bury that cove deep enough for me, an older man named Parton said, and those sharing the store bench with him nodded in agreement. When he asked why, Parton muttered that the cove was a place where only bad things happened. He left the men on the bench and walked back to his truck. He was used to these rural people and their superstitions, even written some down to share with other TVA staff.

He checked his directions and drove out of Mars Hill, passing the college that shared the town's unusual name. A banner draped over the entrance gate proclaimed WELCOME FUTURE CLASS OF 1957. *The road rose and then made a slow descent before rising again. He parked where two slashes of blue paint brightened a post oak's trunk and walked half a mile up a washout to the deserted farmhouse whose last inhabitant, at least according to the courthouse records in Marshall, was a man named Slidell Hampton. A barn sagged nearby, next to it a family cemetery high enough that the graves need not be moved. Time and weather had erased all the names and dates except on two marble stones. He took out his handkerchief and wiped the sweat off his face, wished he'd brought the canteen left in the truck.*

Beyond the farmhouse, another marked tree showed the way into the cove. At first what he followed was more the memory of a trail, places where weeds and saplings grew instead of trees, but as he moved downward the granite cliff narrowed and an old path emerged. Where the land leveled for a few yards, an ash tree rose on the left, one thick limb leaning into the cliff. Bottles and tin scraps hung from the limb like wind chimes. Shards of colored glass and yellow salt from a cow lick littered the ground. He'd seen a similar collage in Tennessee, been told its purpose was to keep evil from coming through.

He passed under the limb and the land fell sharply. The cliff loomed over him now, the trail's surface more granite than dirt. The land leveled a last time and he walked into a stand of dead chestnut trees, their limbs broken off, massive trunks cracked as though a plague of lightning had swept through the cove. The cabin still stood, flanked on its sides by two wells, only one with a rope and pulley. Rusty sags of barbed wire outlined a pasture that held nothing but briar and broom sedge. Collapsed boards smothered the barn's cor-

belled foundation. No sign of any recent human presence, which was all for the better. All he'd have to do was a quick deed search.

He sat on the porch steps and checked his watch and then looked at the cliff face. The upper portion leaned inward and blocked half the sky. With the opposite ridge high as well, the cove was submerged in shadow even though it was midafternoon. He thought how little this place would change once underwater. Already dark and silent. An ornithologist claimed this area might hold the last Carolina Parakeets in the world, but he couldn't imagine anything that bright and colorful ever being here.

His eyes resettled on the well with the pulley. Its bucket was rust pocked, the rope a gray unraveling, but worth a try, so he left the porch. At first the crank wouldn't turn, and he had to use both hands before the lock of rust yielded and the bucket made its swaying descent. The rope whitened as it unspooled. The handle and winch flaked scabs of rust as the bucket kept falling. Probably dry, he thought, but when the rope slackened and he made a tentative crank in the opposite direction, he felt the weight of water. He turned the handle a few more times before the bucket snagged.

At first he assumed a branch that the wind had tumbled into the well, then a root when the obstruction stubbornly clutched the bucket's rim. He gave a jerk and the bucket rose again, coming up and up and finally emerging into what light the cove offered. He slackened the rope and swung the bucket away from the hole and set it on the ground. There was more than he'd expected, the bucket two-thirds full, but the water was murky. Let it settle a minute, he thought, and then you can decide how thirsty you are. He looked at the cliff and imagined water inching up it day by day, week by week, month by month. Like the tip on an iceberg, there would be a small part of the cliff that wouldn't be underwater. People would have no inkling it was once immense enough to shadow a whole cove. He looked back into the pail, the water still cloudy but clearing enough to see something else harbored in the bucket's bottom. He thought it might be his own dim reflection. Then the water cleared more and what lay in the bucket assumed a round and pale solidity, except for the holes where the eyes had been.

I

CHAPTER ONE

At first Laurel thought it was a warbler or thrush, though unlike any she'd heard before—its song more sustained, as if so pure no breath need carry it into the world. Laurel raised her hands from the creek and stood. She remembered the bird Miss Calicut had shown the class. A Carolina Parakeet, Miss Calicut had said, and unfolded a handkerchief to reveal the green body and red and yellow head. Most parakeets live in tropical places like Brazil, Miss Calicut explained, but not this one. She'd let the students pass the bird around the room, telling them to look closely and not forget what it looked like, because soon there'd be none left, not just in these mountains but probably in the whole world.

Sixteen years since then, but Laurel remembered the long tail and thick beak, how the green and red and yellow were so bright they seemed to glow. Most of all she remembered how light the bird felt inside the handkerchief's cool silk, as if even in death retaining the weightlessness of flight. Laurel couldn't remember if Miss Calicut described the parakeet's song, but what she heard now seemed a fitting match, pretty as the parakeets themselves.

As Laurel rinsed the last soap from her wash, the song merged with the water's rhythms and the soothing smell of rose pink and bee balm. She lifted Hank's army shirt from the pool and went to where the granite outcrop leaned out like a huge anvil. Emerging from the mountain's vast shadows was, as always, like stepping from behind a curtain. She winced from the sunlight, and her bare feet felt the strangeness of treading a surface not aslant. The granite was warm and dry except on the far side where the water flowed, but even there the creek slowed and thinned, as if it too savored the light and was reluctant to enter the cove's darkness.

Laurel laid Hank's shirt near the ledge and stretched out the longer right sleeve first, then the other. She looked around the bedraped granite, her wash like leavings from the stream's recent flooding. Laurel raised her chin and closed her eyes, not to hear the bird but to let the sun immerse her face in a warm waterless bath. The only place in the cove she could do this, because the outcrop wasn't dimmed by ridges and trees. Instead, the granite caught and held the sunlight. Laurel could be warm here even with her feet numbed by the creek water. Hank had built a clothesline in the side yard but she didn't use it, even in winter. Clothes dried quicker in the sunlight and they smelled and felt cleaner, unlike the cove's depths where clothes hung a whole day retained a mildewed dampness.

They'll dry just as quick if I ain't watching, Laurel told herself, and set down the wicker basket. She remembered how Becky Dobbins, a store owner's daughter, asked why the farmer killed such a pretty bird. Because they'll eat your apples and cherries, Riley Watkins had answered from the back row. Anyway, they're the stupidest things you ever seen, Riley added, and told how his daddy fired into a flock and the unharmed parakeets didn't fly away but kept circling until not one was left alive. Miss Calicut had shaken her head. It's not because they're stupid, Riley.

Laurel followed the creek's ascent, stepping around waterfalls and rocks and felled trees when she had to, otherwise keeping her feet in water and away from any prowling copperhead or satinback. The land steepened and the water blurred white. Oaks and tulip poplars dimmed the sun and rhododendron squeezed the banks tighter. Laurel paused and listened, the bird's call rising over the water's rush. They never desert the flock, Miss Calicut had told them, and Laurel had never known it to be otherwise. On the rarer and rarer occasions the parakeets passed over the cove, they always flew close together. Sometimes they called to one another, a sharp cry of *we we we*. A cry but not a song, because birds didn't sing while flying. The one time a flock lit in her family's orchard, the parakeets had no chance to sing.

But this parakeet, if that's what it was, did sing, and it sang alone. Laurel sidled around another waterfall. The song became louder, clearer, coming not from the creek but near the ridge crest. As quietly as possible, Laurel left the water and made her way through trees twined with virgin's bower, then into a thicket of rhododendron. Close now, the song's source only a few yards away. On the thicket's other side, sunlight fell through a breech in the canopy. Laurel crouched and moved nearer, pulled aside a last thick-leaved rhododendron branch. A flash of silvery flame caused her to scuttle back into the thicket, brightness pulsing on the back of her eyelids.

The song did not pause. She blinked until the brightness went away and again moved closer, no longer crouching but on her knees. Through a gap in the leaves she saw a haversack, then shoes and pants. Laurel lifted her gaze, her eyelids squinched to shutter the brightness.

A man sat with his back against a tree, eyes closed as his fingers skipped across a silver flute. All the while his cheeks pursed and puffed, nostrils flaring for air. The man's blond hair was a greasy tangle, his whiskers not yet a full beard but enough of one to, like his hair, snare dirt and twigs. Laurel let her gaze take in a blue chambray shirt torn and frayed and missing buttons, the corduroy pants ragged as the shirt, and shoes whose true color was lost in a lathering of dried mud. Sunday shoes, not brogans or top overs. Except for the flute, whatever else the man possessed looked to be in the haversack. A circle of black ground and charred wood argued he'd been on the ridge at least a day.

The song ended and the man opened his eyes. He set the flute across his raised knees and tilted his head, as though awaiting a response to the song. Perhaps one he would not welcome, because he appeared suddenly tense. His eyes swept past Laurel and she saw that no crow's feet crinkled the eyes, the brow and cheeks briar scratched but unlined. The eyes were the same blue as water in a deep river pool, the face long and thin, features more hewn than kneaded. Laurel tugged the muslin on her left shoulder closer to her neck. Then he closed his eyes again and pressed his lower lip to the metal, played something more clearly a human song.

Up this high, the rhododendron blossoms hadn't fully wilted. Their rich perfume and the vanilla smell of the virgin's bower made Laurel light-headed as minutes passed and one song blended into another. The sun leaned west and what light the gap in the trees allowed sifted away. The flute's sparkling silver muted to gray but the music retained its airy brightness.

It felt like she'd listened only a few minutes, but when Laurel got back to the outcrop Hank's shirt was almost dry. She gathered the socks and step-ins, her other muslin work dress, and Hank's overalls. A purple butterfly lit on the stream edge to sip water. A pretty hue, most anyone would say, the same way they'd speak of church glass or bull thistle as pretty. Just not pretty on white skin, though she hadn't known the difference until first grade. When she was eight, the taunts had gotten so bad that she'd scrubbed the birthmark with lye soap until the skin blistered and bled. With that memory came another, of Jubel Parton. Laurel placed the one-wristed army shirt in the basket last, its damp shadow lingering on the granite. Up on the ridge, the music stopped.

He could be coming down the creek, Laurel realized, maybe glimpsed her through the trees. For the first time, she felt a shiver of fear. As beautiful as the music had been, the man's scratched face and tattered clothes argued trouble, perhaps a tramp looking for a farmhouse to rob. Maybe do worse than just steal, she thought. Laurel looked toward the ridge and listened for the crunch of leaves. The only sound was the murmur of the stream. The music resumed, coming from the same place on the ridge.

She pressed the wicker basket against her belly and made her way down the trail. The air grew dank and dark and even darker as she passed through a stand of hemlocks. Toadstools and witch hazel sprouted on the trail edge, farther down, nightshade and then baneberry whose poisonous fruit looked like a doll's eyes. Two days' rain had made the woods poxy with mushrooms. The gray ones with the slimy feel of slugs were harmless, Laurel knew, but the larger pale mushrooms could kill you, as could the brown-hooded kind that clumped on rotting wood. Chestnut wood, because that was what filled the understory more and more with each passing season. As Laurel approached her parents' graves, she thought of what she'd asked Slidell to do, what he said he'd do, though adding that at his age such a vow was like snow promising to outlast spring.

Laurel set the basket down and stood in front of the graves. One was fifteen years old, the other less than a year, but the names etched on the soapstone had been lichened to a similar gray-green smoothness. Laurel knew those who avoided this cove would see some further portent in such vanishing. But the barbed wire and colt and calves were portents too, good portents, though the best was Hank surviving the war when most people believed this place marked him for sure death. But Hank hadn't died. Missing a hand, but other men from outside the cove had fared much worse. Paul Clayton had been in a Washington hospital for two months and Vince Ford and Wesley Ellenburg had come home in flag-draped coffins. Soon Hank was going to get married, another good thing.

It would be an adjustment deciding who cooked or who cleaned, who swept the floors or drew the water. There'd be times she and Carolyn might get huffy with each other, but they'd figure it out. They'd become like sisters after a while. Carolyn was a reader, Hank had said, everything from her daddy's newspaper to books, so they'd have that in common. As Laurel left the woods, she saw Hank and Slidell stretching barbed wire in the upper pasture. Eighty-one, but Slidell tried to help Hank an hour or two each day. With so many men conscripted, hired hands were scarce, those few around unwilling to work in the cove. Only Slidell would, and he refused money, only took an occasional favor in return. She watched as Hank set the wire in the crowbar's claw and pulled against the brace, enough strength garnered in that one arm and hand to stretch the strand tight as a fiddle string. Hank's right bicep was twice as big as the left, the forearm thick and ropy with blue veins that bulged with each pull. He was so much stronger than when he'd first returned from Europe. Strong enough that even one armed, no one, including Jubel Parton, would want to cross him.

Laurel stopped at the springhouse and set a quart jar of sweet milk and a cake of butter atop the clothes. Past time to start supper, but once on the porch she lingered and watched the men work. The pasture fence was nearly a quarter done, the wire strung and the locust posts deep rooted and straight, more proof to Carolyn's father, who sometimes watched from the notch head, that even with one hand Hank could support a wife and children. Hank remained tight lipped about his exact plans, the way he was about a lot of things, but last month Laurel had passed his room and seen him studying what their mother had called the wish book, a pencil in his hand. Later she'd taken the thick catalog off of Hank's bureau and found the pages he'd corner-folded. Penciled stars marked a Provider six-hole cast-iron range, Golden Oak chiffonier, and Franklin sewing machine. She'd been about to close the wish book when she saw another fold. This page showed a three-quarter-carat diamond ring. Beside the words *Must include ring size* Hank had written *6*.

Laurel went inside. She took the dough tray off its peg and set it on the cook table. As she opened the meal gum and scooped out flour with the straight cup, Laurel debated whether to tell Hank and Slidell about the man with the flute, decided not to.

CHAPTER TWO

When Laurel awoke on Saturday, she busied herself with the morning chores, cleaning out the ash grate, fetching milk and butter from the spring-house, water from the well. Hank had laid wood and kindling in the firebox last night, so she stuffed a page from last year's wish book inside and raked a kitchen match across the black iron. The fire caught and Laurel clanged the door shut. The warm smell of coffee filled the room as she fried the eggs and slid them on the plates, took cornbread from the pie safe and placed it on the table by the blackberry jam and butter, milk for the coffee. Last month Hank had wondered aloud if they should buy a shoat to raise for breakfast meat. He'd shown no surprise when Laurel argued against it.

Even before the parakeets had come to the cove, the chore Laurel hated most growing up was feeding the hogs. There had been three in the pen, one a shoat but the others thick and hairy and tall as calves. Each time Laurel fed them, she'd approached with shaking hands, moving quietly so she could pour the slops before the hogs rushed the trough. But they always knew. When she leaned the pail over the top board, the hogs squealed and grunted, clambered into the wooden trough and crashed their swollen bodies against the board slats. The gray wood bowed and the rusty nails creaked and each time Laurel believed the boards and nails would give and the hogs would tear her apart like a poppet doll.

Hank cursed and Laurel knew some button or snap frustrated him, that or a bootlace. Things he wouldn't let her help him with. He came out wearing the shirt she'd washed yesterday, the left sleeve cut off at the elbow so he'd not have to bother pinning it. She poured the coffee and they sat down to eat. There was a fairness in not telling about the man with the flute, Laurel thought, because Hank kept so much to himself, especially about Carolyn Weatherbee. He was all but betrothed, if not betrothed, but Laurel knew nothing about the wedding plans.

Her daddy's a superstitious old fool and I got to humor him since he's already tallied my gone hand against me. That was how Hank explained never asking Laurel along on Sunday mornings when he borrowed Slidell's horse and wagon and made the three-mile trip to the Weatherbee farm, or how, at the victory jubilees, Hank barely acknowledged Laurel once the Weatherbees arrived. That'll soon change, she reminded herself. What the old man believed wouldn't matter once Hank and Carolyn were married and living in the cove.

They didn't speak until only smears of jam remained on their plates.

"I'll go feed the colt and calves," Hank said as he pushed back his chair.

"Slidell helping you today?"

"Probably not. It sounded like he's got a full portion doing his own chores, especially since we're off to town come afternoon."

After Hank left, Laurel washed the cups and dishes and flatware, filled the gray berlin kettle with pole beans and set it on the stove to simmer. She went to the sink, sifted soda powder on her toothbrush and brushed her teeth before she tied her hair back with a crimped hairpin. Dew soaked her bare feet as she walked toward the cornfield. A crow cawed once and lifted from amid the tasseled stalks, passed over the two nailed boards and the tattered remnants of a shirt. She'd need to get another from the bottom drawer, maybe set a straw hat atop the seed-sack face. Might at least keep them from roosting on it, Laurel figured.

The cliff loomed over her and though her eyes were cast downward she felt its presence. Even inside the cabin she could feel it, as though the cliff's shadow was so dense it soaked through the wood. Nothing but shadow land, her mother had told Laurel, and claimed there wasn't a gloamier place in the whole Blue Ridge. A cursed place as well, most people in the county believed, cursed long before Laurel's father bought the land. The Cherokee had stayed away from the cove, and the first white family to settle here had all died of smallpox. There were stories of hunters who'd come into the cove and never been seen again, a place where ghosts and fetches wandered. But Laurel's parents didn't know these things the spring her father crossed the state line separating Cocke County and Madison in search of cheap land, found a hundred acres for the price of twenty in Tennessee.

Laurel was eight when her father collapsed in the field. Doctor Carter had told him there was nothing to be done except not exert himself. Then Laurel's mother had died and after that hardly anyone except Slidell entered the cove. Even Preacher Goins, who'd bibled her mother's funeral, made sure he left before dark. He hadn't taken Laurel's hand or hugged her and Laurel knew the why of that too. At school her classmates echoed what their parents believed—that her father's heart gave out after rocking Laurel with the birthmark touching his chest, that her mother's poisoned limb had turned the color of Laurel's stained skin, that the cove itself had marked Laurel as its own. Superstitions are just coincidence or ignorance. That was what Miss Calicut always told the class when a student said an owl's hoot meant someone would die or killing black snakes could end a drought. But her saying so didn't do much good, especially when parents complained that Miss Calicut needed to stick to reading and ciphering—things a schoolmarm understood.

Laurel laid the hoe at a row end. Hank was in the high pasture, his back to her as he planted another fence post. I'll just go as far as the wash pool, she told herself. As she passed the barn, she saw a praying mantis long as a pencil clinging to a board. At the wood's edge, dark berries sagged the poke stalks and the joe-pye weed was level with her eyes. All sure signs summer would soon be over.

Laurel followed the path through dead chestnuts whose peeling bark revealed wood the color of bone. Cleared four hundred dollars on the deal and we'll be able to live off the chestnuts alone, her father bragged when he bought the land, but red dots sinister as those on black widows had already appeared on the tree trunks. Then as their first summer here passed, more and more dark patches scoured the once-green ridges. One more calamity, because blue mold had rotted the tobacco and the light-starved orchard had yielded only a sprinkling of shriveled fruit. Her father had sworn a blind man would be more fortunate, because he'd at least not have to watch it happen.

When Laurel got to the outcrop, she sat and listened to sounds usually no more noticeable than her own breath. But she heard them now, water swiveling around rocks, the wind stirring leaves, the farther-off pecking of a yellowhammer. All of these she heard first, because the music was quieter today, a mournful song played softly.

Coincidence and ignorance, Miss Calicut said, but there had been times in the last year, especially after her father died, that Laurel felt she herself might be a ghost. Did a ghost even know it was a ghost? Days would pass and Laurel wouldn't see a single living soul. She'd left the cove only on the Saturdays she went to town with Slidell or to the monthly victory jubilees. Both places people avoided her, crossing the street, moving to another barn corner. Wasn't that what a ghost was, a thing cut off from the living? Those nights in the cove Laurel had waked to sounds and silences never noticed when Hank or her father had been around—the emptiness of every other room, the creak of the well's rope and pulley, the cabin resettling some part of itself—the loneliest sorts of sounds and silences. There had been mornings she'd looked in the mirror and wondered if what she saw wasn't a reflection but instead a floating weightless thing. After a while she quit changing the month on the Black Draught calendar. If Slidell showed up in his brogans and overalls to help with chores Laurel couldn't do alone, it was Wednesday. If he wore a white linen shirt and corduroy pants, it was the weekend. Laurel remembered how once she'd leaned close just to see her breath condense on the mirror's glass.

One night at a victory jubilee Jubel Parton asked her to go outside, winking at his friends as he did so. Reeking of whiskey, he kissed her sloppily on the mouth. Doing it because he's drunk, Laurel had believed, but let him do it anyway, because if his hands and lips could touch her, she was yet flesh and blood. Jubel's daddy owned Parton's Outdoor Goods, so the next Saturday when she and Slidell were in Mars Hill, Laurel had walked down an aisle of steel traps and cane poles to the counter. Jubel told another clerk to take the register and led Laurel to the cellar where they lay on burlap feed bags that chafed her arms and legs. She'd have let him have her right then, but after a few minutes he stopped. Need us a rubber so there won't be no woods colt, Jubel had said, and told her he'd bring one to the next jubilee. Three weeks later Jubel was waiting outside. He'd taken a last swallow from a whiskey bottle and handed it to Ray Janson, who snickered as Jubel took Laurel's hand, grabbed a horse blanket from a wagon, and walked to the pasture's edge. There was enough light from the barn mouth to risk being seen and Laurel asked to go into the woods. Better here, Jubel had answered. After they'd finished, Jubel gave her a checkered handkerchief to wash the blood off her legs. It was only when she got up that Laurel saw the others. Jubel walked toward Ray Janson and held out his hand for the wagered gold coin.

As the flute began another song, Laurel thought of how in six months they'd have a horse big enough to haul the wagon. They could start selling milk and eggs, if not in Mars Hill then Marshall, and each year there'd be more livestock. She'd even seen the parakeets last week. A small flock, no more than a half dozen, but they had swooped low enough to show their red and yellow heads before crossing the ridge toward the Ledbetter farm. And this music, another pretty thing that had found its way into the cove. Laurel dipped her hand and felt the shock of cold as she palmed the water and drank. Go on up there or go on home, she told herself, you've got too many chores to dawdle. She stepped into the water and followed the flute's song up the ridge and into the rhododendron.

The stranger was exactly as he'd been yesterday, back against the tree and eyes closed as he balanced the flute. His not moving gave her a chill. Having to eat or drink or stretch your legs was a human thing. Laurel looked around for mushrooms in a fairy ring or some other sign. Expecting the worst of him same as folks do to you, Laurel chided herself. Scabs and scratches proved that the stranger bled. Eating too, for nubbed corncobs lay in the campfire's ashes. Laurel eased herself onto the ground. The song was wistful as the ballads Slidell and the Clayton brothers played, except words weren't needed to feel the yearning. That made the music all the more sorrowful, because this song wasn't about one lost love or one dead child or parent. It was as if the music was about every loss that had ever been.

The man stopped midsong and peered intently down the ridge, then seemed to relax. He placed the flute in the leather case and sat a few minutes, thinking about something. She couldn't tell if what he pondered pleased or vexed him, but Laurel suddenly wished she could know. It would be, like the music, something secretly shared. The man stood and stretched, walked up to the ridge crest and gazed toward the Ledbetter farm. Laurel lifted a rhododendron branch to see his campsite better. A tree branch shaped like a club lay beside the leaf pallet.

One end wasn't much thicker than a tobacco stick, but a burl knot on the other bulged big as a yarn ball. He could have seen a copperhead or heard a panther. It could be for nothing more than that, Laurel told herself, but crept farther back into the rhododendron.

The stranger came down the ridge and took an apple from the haversack. Green and hard, but he bit right into it, his mouth pruning with its sourness. Laurel's stomach grumbled because it was near noon-dinner time for her too, but if she moved he'd hear her. The man finished the apple and threw the core into the woods, picked up the flute. This time the notes were hesitant, more like birdsong. His eyes closed and the notes blended into each other and it wasn't the song of a warbler or peewee but a thrush, the kind with black spots and a reddish tail. Go, Laurel told herself, before he stops again.

As she walked into the yard, Hank checked the pocket watch he'd brought back from France.

"We need to soon get going or Slidell will leave without us," Hank said.

Laurel hurriedly fixed their food and left the dishes for later. She and Hank walked toward the notch, passing through more dead chestnuts. The blight that killed them was first found in New York City, Miss Calicut had told them, but there were people who swore that, in these mountains at least, it had started here in the cove. The land began to slant upward and the cliff's shadow deepened. As the trail thinned, Hank stepped ahead of her. The trail curled around the cliff face and the sky spread out wide and blue as if leveled by a rolling pin.

At the trail notch, an ash tree narrowed the passage. Glass bottles had been knotted to the limb with leather strips, hung close so they could clink against each other, on the wood itself an *X* painted in red. Pieces of glass, some blue and some clear, cluttered the ground like spills of rock candy.

Put there as a warning. Hank cursed and kicked the glass shards off the path, raised wisps of salt as he did so. His shoulders pulled inward and his hand clenched. When he'd first come back from the war, Hank had torn bottles and cans off the branch, but they always reappeared. He paused and Laurel thought he might strip the tree again. Instead, Hank went on and Laurel followed.

"Hope we didn't hold you up," Hank said as they came into the yard.

"Naw," Slidell said.

He raised himself from the porch steps, picked up his shotgun, and began walking toward the barn. Slidell's face was chapped and deep furrowed, but he moved with the gait of a man decades younger. Shoulders unhunched, belly taut and hazel eyes clear. Even the white hair was spry, thick and bristly. Hank followed Slidell to the barn to help harness Ginny to the wagon. Laurel waited in the side yard by the bee box. A drowsy hum came from inside the white wood. One day soon Slidell would smoke the bees, take out the super, and pour the honey into quart mason jars. He'd bring Hank and Laurel more than he'd keep for himself. Laurel would hear him coming, the jars clanking inside a tote sack swung over his shoulder.

She joined the men on the buckboard and Slidell gathered the checkreins in his gnarly hands. They bumped down a wide path, passing the small graveyard and the pasture, once a cornfield, where Slidell's father and brother had been killed by outliers during the Confederate War. Folks will step on my land and not fret a moment that a man and a fourteen-year-old boy was murdered here with less conscience than killing two snakes,

Slidell had once told her. This is a place folks ought to be scared of, not some gloamy cove.

Soon the path spread its weedy shoulders and became a dirt wayfare. The land slanted downward and trees thickened. Ginny was old and swaybacked, her gait slow and measured. Slidell gave the checkreins an occasional halfhearted shake, more out of habit than expectation the horse's pace would quicken.

Hank nodded at the double-barreled shotgun in the wagon bed.

"That boar hog vexing you again?"

"No, but last week he was standing bold as Jehoshaphat at the end of this wayfare. He didn't look to be trifled with, especially with those tusks jutting off his face like hay hooks."

"But you haven't seen him near the notch?" Laurel asked.

"Not yet, but come near harvesttime I figure him to make his way up to my cabbage patch like he done last year, unless that shotgun curbs his appetite once and for all."

"I hope you kill it," Laurel said.

"Help me be on the lookout and maybe I'll satisfy the both of us," Slidell said. He jostled the checkreins again and turned to Hank. "You buying more wire today?"

"That and staples," Hank answered. "I might price a pulley for the new well, in case I ever get the damn thing done."

"I wish I could help you," Slidell said, "but well digging is a young man's game, at least far deep as you are now. This war will end soon and there'll be more young men around. They'll have been out in the world and be less obliged to listen to tall tales and nonsense."

"Maybe," Hank said.

They came to the old Marshall toll pike and turned left. Wheel tracks from wagons and automobiles braided the dust and chert. The trees were not as close or numerous. They passed several cabins, then a two-story farmhouse whose tin roof shimmered. More homes appeared and fewer fields and pastures. Laurel could see the college now, first the clock tower and then the brick and wood buildings. The pike crested a last time and they descended, first passing the granite arch and brick drive that led up to the college, then coming into town.

As always, Laurel felt her stomach tense. Since it was Saturday, wagons and horses were tethered to every hitching post, a few automobiles nosed up to the boardwalks as well. The wagon made a halting progress amid farm families and town folk, a few college students. Laurel looked for Marcie Bettingfield's wagon, hoping to hear how she and her baby were doing. They passed Lusk's Barbershop and Feith Savings and Loan, across from them what had been a tailor's shop but now had UNITED STATES RECRUITING OFFICE painted on the window. Chauncey Feith stood outside the doorway in his uniform. Laurel glanced over to see if Hank noticed him, but his eyes were fixed straight ahead, as were hers when they passed Parton's Outdoor Goods.

Two women in bonnets came out of the post office. One nudged the other at the wagon's approach. They hurriedly crossed the street, heads turned so the bonnets concealed their faces. Slidell found an empty hitching post in front of the spinning red-and-white pole advertising Lusk's Barbershop.

"You all take your time," Slidell said as they got off the buckboard. "After I get my trading done, I'll be at the Turkey Trot. Just come get me when you're ready."

"What do you need to buy, sister?" Hank asked after Slidell left.

"Just knitting and sewing doings, and maybe look at some cloth."

"Dawdle awhile if you got a mind to," Hank said as they stepped onto the boardwalk. "After I get my wire and staples I'm going to talk to Neil Lingefelt about that pulley."

A farm woman in a flour-cloth dress came up the boardwalk. When she stepped into the street so as not to pass near them, Hank's face tightened.

"I need to go," he said.

"I'll help you carry stuff to the wagon," Laurel said, "before I go to the cloth shop."

"No," Hank said quickly. "Erwin's boy will help me."

She watched Hank walk up the boardwalk. He paused to shake hands with Marvin Alexander and was greeted with a nod and smile by a passing couple. In those two years they'd been in school together, it had been hard for both of them but worse for Laurel because of the birthmark. Yet she and Hank had never allowed any difference. At school, he'd fight boys older and bigger because of remarks just aimed at Laurel. Once something started, she'd done the same for him, clawing and biting anyone who took on Hank. Then Ellie Anthony, who sat near them, came down with polio. Her parents claimed Laurel and Hank the cause. Other parents vowed to keep their children out of school until Laurel and Hank were gone.

On trips to town after that, they'd been treated even worse. Besides the snubs and glares they'd grown used to, some people spat as she and Hank went by. A man threatened to horsewhip Slidell if he kept bringing them to town and one Saturday she and Hank had been hit by rotten eggs. Bad as it was, they'd at least endured it together, but since Hank's return from Europe, most of the meanness had been directed only at Laurel. More than a hand had been left behind in Europe, people seemed to believe.

Laurel walked across the street to the cloth shop. The bell

above the door jingled as Laurel entered. Becky Dobbins's mother, Cordelia, raised her eyes and frowned before turning back to writing in a ledger. Laurel picked up a buying basket and put in three spools of sewing thread and a pack of fish-eye buttons. The muslin she wanted to price was next to the counter, but Laurel slowly made her way amid the various bolts of cloth, the reds and blues and yellows and colors mixed and between, a whole school globe's worth of color. Laurel thought of the stranger's shabby clothes and paused before a thick bolt of denim. She wondered if he was playing the silver flute right now.

Laurel went over to the window where dress cloth hung from wood rods like bright flags. She lingered among the linen and serge, the tussah silk that was always cool to the touch. She raised cloth ends to better see the prettiness of the checks and stripes and solids.

"Appreciate it if you don't handle that cloth," Mrs. Dobbins said, "unless you're of a mind to buy it."

Laurel paid for the thread and buttons and went back outside, her eyes blinking as they adjusted to the light. Hank had loaded the last of the thorny wheels of barbed wire in the wagon and was in front of the barbershop talking to Ben Lusk. All the times Laurel had been in town, the barber had never acknowledged her with a word or even a nod. Ben laughed at something Hank said and playfully slapped him on the shoulder. She stepped onto the boardwalk and caught Hank's eye.

"What is it?" Hank asked, coming over to her.

"There's something I've been needing to tell you," Laurel said.

"Why in hell didn't you tell me this before?" Hank seethed when she'd finished.

Laurel didn't answer, just watched as Hank's face seemed to waver between anger and resignation. Slidell came up the boardwalk with a tote sack in his hand. He was about to set it in the wagon when he saw Hank's face.

"What's the matter?" Slidell asked, but Hank was already stepping off the boardwalk and headed toward Parton's Outdoor Goods.

Slidell looked at Laurel.

"What is it?"

"There's going to be a fight," Laurel said.

"I need to stop this," Slidell said, but it was too late.

Jubel came reeling out of the store's front door, Hank right behind. The men clinched and hit the boardwalk together and rolled over twice. Hank came up on top and drove a fist into Jubel's face. Blood spouted from Jubel's nose as Hank cocked his elbow to swing again, but bystanders were already untangling them, ensuring the men were well apart before helping each to his feet. Jubel wiped a forearm over his nose and upper lip, gauged the blood on his shirt.

"I reckon it's still worth a gold quarter eagle," he said.

Hank broke free and swung again, nicking Jubel's chin. Slidell and Tillman Estep pulled Hank away and Chauncey Feith stepped between the two combatants.

"We can't be tussling amongst ourselves when we have Huns to fight," Chauncey admonished.

"What would you know about fighting Huns, Feith?" Hank answered.

Chauncey Feith raised a hand and ever so slowly adjusted the bill of his army cap, but it did not hide his flushed face as the boardwalk filled with more gawkers. A woman Laurel did not know gave Jubel a damp handkerchief.

"You want me to send someone for Doctor Carter?" Feith asked.

"Hell, no," Jubel replied, nodding at his sleeve. "This ain't nothing."

"Okay then," Chauncey Feith said, and turned to the gawkers. "We've got this settled so let's all be about our business."

Jubel was escorted back into the store.

"Time for us to go," Slidell said.

She and Hank followed Slidell across the street to the wagon. As they passed back through town, a man in overalls muttered at Laurel and spat.

"Why didn't you tell me sooner?" Hank asked once they were past the college.

"I was shameful of it," Laurel said.

"Yeah, I guess you would be," Hank said, no warmth in his voice. "You know about this, Slidell?"

"No."

Slidell lifted a rein to wipe a dribble of tobacco off his mouth, looking straight ahead as he spoke.

"But it's something you'll have to get past, the both of you."

"I'm tired of having to get past stuff," Hank answered. "I've been doing that all my life."

"But you ain't the only one who's had to," Slidell said.

"I ain't forgot what happened to you," Hank said.

"I wasn't talking about me," Slidell answered.

For a few moments the only sounds were the squeak of the springs and axle, the soft clap of iron horseshoes on dirt.

"I know that too," Hank said, not looking at Laurel or Slidell but straight ahead.

CHAPTER THREE

Every evening for a week the old man had walked down the path to the river. A tin bait bucket swayed in his hand and a stringer was tied loosely around his neck. The rest of his gear lay hidden in the high grass a few yards from the wooden rowboat. He would set the oars in the bow, then place the lantern and hooks and ball of string on the boat's planking and push off. Once in the river, the old man checked lines he had hung from willow branches. Hand over fist, he pulled straight up as if drawing water from a well. Sometimes trout and carp thrashed to the surface, but more often what emerged were blunt-headed fish whose dark bodies tapered like comets. The fisherman sewed the stringer through a gill and pulled the loop tight before dropping his catch back in the river. He would rebait the hooks and paddle to the next line. This evening, as was his habit, the old man was back ashore by dusk. He trudged up the path, his body keeled rightward by the stringer's heft, fishtails thickening with dust.

Walter watched until the fisherman passed the guard tower, then turned from the fence and went inside the barracks, making his way past men playing cards and pinochle, others smoking or writing letters. He lay on his bunk and waited, remembering what the guards had said—that the easy part would be getting over the fence. Finding the way out of these wild mountains would be the challenge. But with the fisherman's boat, he would not be wandering dense forests but following a current that went exactly where he needed to go, and with no trail for dogs to follow.

It was after midnight when Walter stepped out of the barracks' door. In his right hand was a haversack that held the case and flute, a box of matches, the medallion and chain. Tucked in his pocket, the note and the money. Floodlights cast a thick white light over the stockade but no face peered from the guard tower. He waited in the barracks' shadow until the outside guard passed, then scurried to the mesh-wire fence and began to climb. At the top barbed wire snared his pants. He ripped the cloth free and jumped, hit the ground and dared not look back. As the stockade's lights shallowed behind him, the moon and stars revealed the boat. He shoved off and rowed as fast as he could toward the river's center.

Once in the main current, he pointed the bow downstream toward a place called Asheville. The biggest town in the region, the guards claimed. He would steal some clothes and then find the depot and buy his ticket. Two nights from now he could be back in New York.

Walter rowed rapidly until the stockade lights faded into darkness. Heavy armed and gasping, he eased his pace, allowed himself to savor the river's vastness after so long in confinement. The river made a leisurely curve, then became wider, shallower, rocks sprouting midriver. The dark water gurgled, slapped softly against the largest obstructions. Then the banks tucked themselves closer together and the river deepened. For a while there was no light except what leaked from the sky, then a square of yellow from a farmhouse window, farther on a fisherman's lantern tingeing the shallows. A dog barked. He passed other habitations whose occupants slept, houses unseen though he drifted only a few oar lengths from their doors.

Rested, he began rowing harder. The river widened and then narrowed again. A black panel slid over the sky, locked into place a moment, then slid back, the moon and stars above once more. He turned and saw a bridge's silhouette, high and solid as a ship's hull. The river ran straight for a long while and no lanterns glowed from shore or window, the world absent but for water. He was near exhaustion but did not slacken his pace. The river shallowed, more scrapes and grabs against the planks. He struggled free from the obstructions, angled the bow into seams and squeezed through, bumping and swaying. When he finally came to deeper water, he let go of the oars and leaned forward, head on folded arms and knees. Just for a moment.

Willow branches brushed him awake, the boat's stern shoaled on the bank. The branches were damp with dew, the stars paling and the moon already gone. He rowed back into the current with quick slapping strokes. The river curved and he passed under another bridge, in the distance the flicker of lights. Silhouettes emerged on the shore—outlines of trees, bulky squares of buildings and houses. He passed a brick edifice with an electric light illuminating the words MARSHALL COAL COMPANY. The water's purling music dimmed amid the crow of a rooster, the cough of an automobile engine. Dawnlight unshackled high branches from the dark.

Walter scanned the bank for a white bedsheet semaphoring a clothesline, saw one, and beached the boat. Mostly children's clothes dangled from the wooden pins, but he found a man's cotton shirt and pair of corduroy pants. Just as he finished changing, a dog began barking inside the house. Lights came on and a face appeared in the window. If Walter could have spoken, he would have offered to pay for the clothes, but because that was not possible, he scrambled down to the water, was adrift before a man wielding a shotgun appeared on the bank. Gray smoke blossomed from the gun barrel. Walter ducked and a hail of pellets landed in the boat's wake. The river curved and he lost sight of the man, for good he thought, but the river straightened. An iron railroad trestle appeared and the man with the shotgun was on it. Walter veered the boat toward the far bank as another downpour of lead hit close by.

He beached the boat and grabbed his haversack, but the bank was nothing but a slant of slick mud. By the time he'd climbed it, the man was thrashing through the undergrowth. A hefty piece of driftwood lay on the bank and Walter picked it up, hit the man flush in the chest when he emerged. The man staggered leftward and slid down the bank and into the river. There was a narrow river trail, but Walter picked up the haversack and plunged through a tangle of briars before making his way across a ridge.

All day he wandered without once hearing or seeing anything human. Rain fell that afternoon and fog rolled over the ground like cold smoke. The trees thickened and the woods became as forlorn as those in a sinister fairy tale, a place where the guards claimed lions and bears and wolves roamed. All manner of poisonous serpents and plants thrived here and no step was safe. Immense watery caverns lay just beneath seemingly firm ground. They could give way and a man fall a hundred feet and then into water so utterly dark that the trout living in it were sightless. Walter wasted three matches trying to light the soggy wood, drank water from puddles but was afraid to eat what berries and mushrooms he saw. Night came and he shivered beneath a rock ledge.

The next afternoon Walter came to a brook and followed it. By then he had begun to feel feverish. A music he'd never heard before rose from the stream. The notes had colors as well as sounds, bright threads woven into the water's flow. Some of that bright water splashed up on the bank. It was green and shimmering and he scooped it up into his palm and it became a feather. Wind rustled the branches and he imagined an armada of zeppelins rubbing the treetops.

He heard a dog bark and thought it might be yet another hallucination, but he staggered up to a ridge crest to be sure. On one side was a farmhouse surrounded by fields and an orchard. On the other, no angled rise but a gray wall suspended over a cove like an iceberg, the cliff's looming presence muting the afternoon sunlight. In the cove's deepest section, directly under the cliff face, a purl of smoke drifted above the trees, but that was at least a furlong away. A dreary place, but a fire couldn't be smelled or seen. He stayed three days and three nights, each dawn stealing apples and corn from the farm, gaining his strength back and allowing his blistered feet to heal. On the fourth morning he decided to leave after breakfast, but as he searched for tinder he slipped on the slantland and tumbled.

Black and yellow insects boiled out of the ground. Only when he reached the ridge crest was he free of the swarm.

He lay on his leaf pallet but the ground fell away and he was adrift. A ship came toward him, one he had seen before. The woman in the green dress stood at the railing, looking out expectantly. She was searching for him.

CHAPTER FOUR

He's probably gone on, Laurel thought.

She had been at the creek for hours without a single note drifting down from the ridge. Hank's shirt and overalls and her muslin work dress and step-ins had dried. Laurel put them in the basket but didn't leave. She sat and watched the water. Bright yellow mayflies hatched where the current slowed, the insects blooming on the surface, struggling a few moments, then aloft. They rose and fell, dapping the surface to lay their eggs. One landed on Laurel's arm, and she studied the fragile body, the wings clear and thin as mica flakes. Late in the year for them, but pretty to see. She watched the mayfly drift upward like a spark, fall slowly back to light on the water.

Laurel wished she'd gotten to the outcrop in the morning, but not long after Hank left for the Weatherbees', Slidell had shown up with milk and some creasy greens and stayed for noon-dinner. With each additional minute of silence, the ragged man with the silver flute seemed more impossible. She checked the sky and guessed four o'clock. Hank would be back soon, maybe already was. I've got to touch where that fire was, Laurel thought. If ash rubs black on my hand, at least I'll know he was real, not something my lonesomeness imagined.

She made her way up the creek and into the rhododendron thicket, crouched and lifted a branch. The man lay shivering on the pallet of leaves, his face bright as fireweed. He hardly looked the same person. But he was, the scraggly beard and lank blond hair, the same blue shirt. Laurel moved nearer, close enough to see individual welts amid the swelling. Yellowjacket or hornet stings, more than she'd ever seen on anyone. Too sick to vex me even if he had a mind to, she told herself, so stepped into the clearing and stood above him.

"We need to get you to the cabin," Laurel said. "If I help get you up, can you walk?"

The man opened his eyes as much as the swelling allowed. He looked as if about to speak, but he only nodded. The man grimaced and tried to clench his teeth, but the shivering caused them to tap together.

"Okay, then," Laurel said.

She got him to a sitting position, paused to catch her breath, and helped the stranger to his feet. The man nodded at his haversack.

"I'll get it later. Hoisting you back is chore enough."

They followed the creek down to the path, her hand firm

on his elbow, sidling slightly ahead to better prop him up. Laurel remembered the washed clothes but like the haversack they could wait. The man still didn't speak and she wondered if even the inside of his mouth was swollen. He leaned more of his weight into her, his skin and clothes reeking.

"It ain't far now," she told him as the cabin finally came into sight.

Laurel shouted Hank's name in hopes he was back. A few moments later he came from the barn. He walked rapidly at first, then came running.

"What the hell?" Hank said when he got to them.

"Help me get him to the cabin," Laurel said.

Hank studied the man, not the swollen face but the tattered shirt and pants.

"He looks to be nothing but a tramp come to steal something."

"No, he ain't," Laurel said.

"What is he then?"

"I don't know, but he's more than that, some kind of music player. He's near stung to death."

Hank lifted a red handkerchief from his back pocket. The cloth covered his face as he wiped sweat from his brow and eyes. When he lowered the cloth, Hank looked disappointed that the stranger was still before him.

"All right, but he's not getting inside the cabin till he's had a bath. He stinks."

"Take hold of him," Laurel said. "I'll go fill the tub with water."

Hank placed the man's arm over his right shoulder, settled his hand on the stranger's back as Laurel went on ahead. She set the washtub on the porch and poured in buckets of water until the well's slim holdings grew muddy. She stirred in a handful of Borax before going inside for a washrag and cake of lye soap. Hank sat the man on the front steps and Laurel untied his shoes while Hank helped the stranger take off his shirt.

"Who are you?" Hank asked.

"I think his throat's too swoll to talk," Laurel said, pulling free the second sock. "Help him get his pants and step-ins off while I make a salve."

Laurel nodded at Hank's back pocket.

"I'll need some of your tobacco."

"This is all I got until Slidell goes to town again," Hank grumbled, but handed her the drawstring pouch.

Laurel went in the front room and took the box of soda powder off the sink. She scooped two tablespoons into a rinsing pan, then tucked a wad of tobacco in her mouth and chewed, grimacing all the while. She mixed the tobacco and powder until it was a brown paste, then got the tin of black colish from the cooking shelf and made a tonic with water from the kettle. After fetching a towel and a pair of her father's longhandles, she went out on the porch.

"Damn, sister. We don't know the least thing about him and you're fussing over him like he's the king of England."

"We know he's hurt," Laurel answered, "and we know there's not another near to help him."

She glanced toward the tub, let her eyes linger when she saw the man's eyes were closed. The welts on his neck and chest argued at least as much poison as a copperhead bite. It just wasn't in one place, which Laurel figured a good thing. The water had turned gray from the grime, but the effort had taken what pertness the man had left. The washrag lay limp in his hand.

"You're going to need to lather his hair."

"Do I need to spit shine his shoes too?" Hank answered.

"Hurry, and then get him dressed," Laurel said. "We need to draw out that poison."

In a few minutes Hank helped the man inside. His eyes were open as Hank eased him into the bed. Laurel propped his head up with a feather pillow and held the cup as he sipped the tonic.

"We'll work our way up," she told him when the cup was empty.

Laurel pinched some of the paste between her finger and thumb and covered the first sting, found seven more before she reached the hands and wrists. She freed the longhandles' top buttons to salve his stomach and chest, last his neck and face.

"Damn if he don't look like a bobcat for the spots on him," Hank said when she finished.

"Twenty-one stings," Laurel said. "That's enough to have killed some folks."

"You able to talk yet?" Hank asked, but the man shook his head again.

"Let him be, Hank. He needs to rest."

Despite the warm tonic, the man was trembling, so Laurel spread a quilt over him.

"His clothes have got need of washing, and I need to get ours, so I'm going to be at the creek a spell."

"So what am I supposed to do?" Hank asked. "Stay here all the while so he don't rob us blind?"

"He's not got the sand to do that. Besides, I'll have something he cares a sight more about than anything we got."

"I'm at least taking the shotgun with me," Hank said. "I'd as lief not have him beading its barrel on me."

Laurel looked at the man. His eyes were more alert now, watchful.

"If you got need of the privy, are you able enough to go alone?"

The stranger seemed not to understand.

"Maybe you call it a doaks or outhouse," Laurel said and the man nodded. "It's out behind the cabin."

The man nodded again. Hank took the shotgun from where it leaned in the corner.

"I've got to finish feeding and watering them calves," Hank said, and went out the door.

For a minute Laurel stayed by the bed. The shivering stopped and the man's eyes closed. His breath slowed and steadied into sleep. She studied the stranger's face but found nothing that might tell her more. His left hand lay on the quilt, no knuckles scarred, no fingers stoved or bent from old breaks. Not a farmer or blacksmith, that much was for sure.

Laurel gathered the stranger's clothes in her arms and went outside. Hank was walking toward the barn with the shotgun in his hand and a pail of water crooked in his elbow. In four months he had learned to do things one-handed she'd have not thought possible. He could drive a nail and work a posthole digger, rope a calf, and most anything else you had need for on a farm. He hadn't been the least mewlsome when he came back from France but had dug in his boot heels and gotten on with his life, whether it was farmwork or sparking Carolyn Weatherbee. Hank could get contrary buttoning a shirt or trying to lift a cistern or some such, but it never festered in him.

When she got to the outcrop, Laurel worked the lye soap into the shirt and socks as gently as she could, but the cloth gave apart easy as wisps on a dandelion. Laurel did the pants last. Checking the back pockets, she found three folded twenty-dollar bills, within them a folded piece of butcher paper. She hesitated, but decided she'd earned the right.

> The bearer of this note is Walter Smith.
> A childhood affliction has made him not able to speak.
> He wishes to buy a train ticket to New York City.

Laurel set the note with the money before dipping the pants into the creek. As she doused them for a final rinse, Laurel felt something else in the watch pocket. A coin she thought at first, because it was round like a wheat penny. But what she pulled out was a medallion strung on a thin chain. Circling the medallion's outer edge was a single word. Laurel spread the pants on the rock so they'd at least dry a little. She held the medallion and chain in her palm, the metal blinking a bright gold as it caught the late-afternoon sunlight. Like the silver flute, it didn't fit with the ragged clothing. She thought about placing the medallion and chain in the basket with the note and money, but the way it was hidden made it seem a more private thing. Laurel stuffed the gold back in the watch pocket and went up the creek.

At his camp, she opened the haversack and took out the flute case. The burlap contained nothing else but a single green feather. Laurel held the feather a few moments, wondering where he'd found it. Wherever, he'd thought it worth saving, which was a set-apart sort of thing for a man to do. Laurel put the feather and flute case back inside and shouldered the haversack. She gave the campsite a last look around. Nothing except socks too ripped to darn, some uneaten apples. As she made her way back to the outcrop, Laurel saw cardinal flower abloom on the creek bank. She picked some of the red flowers and worried them between her finger and thumb, rubbed the oil on her neck. Farther on, Queen Anne's lace blossomed. Laurel smiled at herself for noticing it. Best see if this first flower works before you got need for the other, she told herself.

Though the cove below was steadily darkening, she let the pants dry a few minutes longer. Laurel sat on the ledge and clasped her knees. When she was seven, she'd found this place while hunting blackberries. As a child, the outcrop had been like a huge hand that lifted her out of the cove's bleakness. Worst of all was the cabin. No matter the time of day or season or how many lamps were lit, it remained a dim place that, as long as Laurel could remember, always smelled of suffering. But up here the wide shelf of granite gathered the sun's light and held it, swaddled Laurel in brightness. The light was like warm honey. Dewdrops on a spider's web held whole rainbows inside them and a fence lizard's tail shone blue as indigo glass. The water sparkled with mica. Sometimes Laurel laid flat on the outcrop so the sun could fall fuller on her, but most of the time, like now, she'd just fold her knees close to her chest with her hands, as if waiting for something or someone to arrive. Waiting. She had been waiting, waiting in the cabin as well as here for her life to begin, *her life*.

A leaky heart. That was what Doctor Carter called it. Laurel had memories of her father baling hay and plowing, of him and Slidell felling a big white oak with a crosscut saw. But that was before the evening her father hadn't come in for supper and Laurel's mother found him near dead in the field. After that, Doctor Carter came once a month and took his stethoscope from the black leather bag, pressed its silver bell against her father's bony chest. Those had been the moments that frightened Laurel most, because there was always a pause when he moved the bell one place and then another, as if unable to locate her father's heartbeat.

Everyone had to do more as he failed away. While their mother fixed breakfast, Hank fed and milked the cow and Laurel fetched eggs and water. Afternoons the two of them plowed fields and rooked hay and mucked the barn and all of whatever else to keep the farm going. Sometimes her father came on the porch and watched, once hobbled out to hitch a plow to the draft horse. After a few minutes, her mother hoisted him back to the cabin, all the while him gasping for breath and sobbing that he was nothing but a burden, that the world couldn't be made a more sorrowful place. But when Laurel was twelve, she and Hank and her father found the lie of that.

Her mother had been chopping firewood and caught a splinter off a piece of kindling. She'd dug the splinter out with a pocketknife, which should have been the cure of it, but the wound swelled with pus. Her mother cut again, deeper, then poured turpentine in it before wrapping the thumb in cheesecloth. The next morning red streaks ran all the way up to her elbow. Hank went to Mars Hill for Doctor Carter, who came that afternoon and lanced the palm. It had been an awful thing to watch as the blade made its cleave through the flesh. Doctor Carter had soaked the hand in Epsom salts, then wrapped it in cotton gauze. You folks don't die easy, he reassured Laurel and Hank. I'd not have given your daddy six months the first time I heard that heart of his halting and hissing, so I'm of a mind your momma will pull through. But she hadn't. Laurel's father cried that life wasn't supposed to be this hard, that a man sickly as he was shouldn't have a wife die on him.

Laurel had resented those words. He'd had a hard life but her father wasn't alone in that. She became the one who cooked her father's meals and dumped his chamber pot and changed his soiled bedsheets. She'd washed him and salved his bedsores. There had been plenty of misery put on Hank's shoulders too. Slidell had helped some but Hank did most of the farmwork, at nine doing a full man's portion. Their parents had managed to hold on to part of the money from selling the Tennessee farm, money they parceled out to buy what they couldn't grow or make themselves.

Yet she and Hank had made it through, in part because they could count on each other. But it was more than just that, Laurel had always believed. It was also knowing that miserable as life was, there was someone else going through the same thing. As long as Hank could stand it, she could too, not just the hard work but the stares and snubs when they went to Mars Hill with Slidell. At night or rainy days or when the snow flew, they'd play cards or checkers or get out the wish book and pretend they had a thousand dollars and take turns picking out things until neither of them had a single penny left. As they got older, evenings Hank would whittle and Laurel would sew or read copies of the *Marshall Sentinel* that Slidell passed on to them. Sometimes she would take out the geography book Miss Calicut had given her and turn to a page and try to imagine such a farther land. But she never could. They were too distant. All the while their father lingered in the back room, more and more needful as the years passed.

Then Hank got conscripted. I'll never see him again, her father lamented, and he'd been right. One morning Laurel came into her father's room and he lay in the bed dead, his eyes open, as if in death still looking for pity. But Hank had come back.

She had never let herself believe he wouldn't. The morning he'd been shot, she had awakened in bed knowing that he had been hurt, but knowing also as the hours passed that he lived, that he would return.

Laurel rose and checked the rags the stranger had worn, found them yet damp. It was near dark but she'd let the outcrop's warmth dry them a few more minutes. She sat back down on the granite and looked out over the cove to the blue mountains.

Waiting for her life to begin. Still waiting a year after her father's death. But now she felt something was about to happen, maybe already had happened, a beginning this stranger might be part of. Laurel took the flute from the case and found the instrument heavier than she'd have reckoned. It seemed queer that music so light and airy could come from such a solid-feeling thing. She held the flute's mouthpiece to her lips. His lips had touched here as well and the thought pleased her. Laurel made a tentative puff before placing fingers over some of the holes. The silver and her breath brought forth a low plaintive note.

CHAPTER FIVE

Except for two trips to the privy, the man did not leave the bed. He slept through supper and had not awakened when she and Hank went to sleep. In the morning, Laurel set Hank's plate and cup before him and took coffee to the stranger.

"This may taste some different from what you're used to. There's chicory mixed in with the store bought."

The man raised his back against the headboard and took the cup. The swelling had gone down and his color was back. The starch was back in him too. His hands didn't tremble when he brought the cup to his mouth. Laurel nodded at the two stacks of clothes on the bureau, his money and the note beside them. The haversack was near the door and she pointed it out as well.

"I got your clothes washed best as I could but they're in a sorry way," Laurel said. "I read the note, so I know you can't talk. But I can tell you hear okay, and if you done that note you can read and write."

The man shook his head.

"You can't?"

He shook his head again.

"Someone else wrote it for you?"

He nodded.

"Well, anyway, I need to get the daubings off you. They've drawn what poison they will. Besides, like Hank said, you don't want to be mistook for a bobcat."

Laurel went to the front room. As she filled a wash pan with water, Hank pushed back his chair and brought his plate and cup to the basin.

"His clothes are rags so I'm going to give him some of Daddy's to wear," Laurel said. "They're too small for you so someone ought to get use out of them."

"Damn, Laurel," Hank said. "We've already doctored him and give him a bed for the night. That's charity enough. How many folks have done anything for us?"

"Slidell has."

"That's one person."

"And that's all we're helping," Laurel answered. "You saw the note, the man can't even talk."

"Okay," Hank said, "but I'm still taking the shotgun with me."

After Hank left, Laurel sweetened her breath with a piece of licorice root and then took the wash pan into the bedroom, set it on the bed. The man closed his eyes as she rubbed scabs of paste off his face and neck. The washrag was thin and she could feel his skin against her fingertips. As Laurel leaned to free the paste from the other side of his neck, her hair brushed his shoulder. She swept it back behind her ear and tugged the dress collar close to her neck. Brash of her to be so near the man, maybe even dangerous now that he was stronger, but she didn't fear him. He'd stolen, but he'd done that out of hunger. More than anything though, she didn't believe anyone who made such beautiful sounds could be dangerous. Laurel set the cloth in the pan.

"I'll let you dab the ones on your hands and belly," Laurel said.

She took overalls, a chambray shirt, and socks from the bureau's bottom drawer.

"After you finish washing, put them on," Laurel said, setting the clothes on the bed. "Come to the front room and I'll have your breakfast."

The blackberry jam and cornbread and butter were still on the table so she set out a plate and knife. Laurel emptied the stove's ash catch and fed more kindling into the firebox. She filled the berlin kettle with snap beans and potatoes to simmer for noon-dinner. Laurel looked around the room and tried to see it the way the stranger might. There wasn't much to make notice of, no pictures or calendars on the wall, no radio or music box. Maybe the Franklin clock with its hands on the ten and two like stilled wings, or the rio lamp also on the fire board, or the woodstove with the word RAVEN embossed on its iron door. He'd notice the two nailed-together crates that held the books Miss Calicut had given her and probably the flour barrel and butter churn beside the washstand. But nothing bright and pretty like the flute.

When he came into the front room, Laurel saw that the overalls were a decent enough fit. She poured him more coffee and a cup for herself and sat down with him. The man acted near starved from how fast he ate the slavered cornbread, but he didn't make notice of wanting more until it was offered. When he'd finally got enough, Laurel filled their coffee cups again.

"My name's Laurel, though I guess there's not much cause to tell you. It's not like you can say it if you had need to, but I still like you knowing, especially now that I know your name. Is that what you answer to, Walter?"

The man nodded.

"My brother's name is Hank. You might not of noticed yesterday but he's only got one hand. He don't complain but his lot in life is the harder for it, at least in most ways. Not being able to talk, that's got to be burdensome too. I'd think it could make you feel a lavish of aloneness. After my daddy died and Hank was over in France, I was here by myself and it was a hard row to hoe. I guess your music helps you to feel less lonesome, but I've never had anything like that."

Laurel hadn't meant to say so much. Walter didn't move his head or shrug his shoulders but he was listening. She could tell by the way he looked at her while she talked. To have someone meet her eyes was as pleasing a thing as him listening, because so many people looked away or past her like she wasn't even there. Her coffee cup was empty and there were plenty of chores to be done, but Laurel decided they could wait a few more minutes.

"I heard you playing your flute the other day. I was down the creek below you. It was the prettiest thing I've ever heard. Sometimes when I was in school we'd do some singing, and there's music at the victory jubilees, but we've never had it here. Daddy and Momma hadn't a fiddle or guitar or the least sort of music maker. Not that we had much to sing about, at least in a happy way. But just hearing music, even the saddest sort of song, lets you know you're not all of every way alone, that someone else has known the likesomeness of what you have. At least that's what I felt when I heard you playing. Does it ever feel such to you?"

Walter let his eyes settle on the coffee cup. Pondering the question in a serious sort of way, she could tell, like it was something he'd thought about before. He looked up and gave a slight nod.

Laurel smiled.

"You might figure it a blessing this morning that you can't talk, because I've got a peck of questions I'd love to ask. If you could write, I'd surely have you wear out both those yellow pencils on the bookshelf yonder. Well, I do know one thing. You sure look better today than yesterday. Are you feeling more your ownself again?"

Walter nodded and raised the cup to his lips and drank the last of the coffee, shook his head when she asked if he wanted more. He gestured toward the back window and stood up. As he walked out to the privy, Laurel took the dishes and knife to the basin. When Walter came back inside, he seemed unsure what to do so lingered near the door. She watched his eyes take in the room, settling on nothing long until he saw Hank's tunic on a peg.

"That's Hank's army coat. I guess you can't be a soldier unless you can speak."

Walter nodded.

"You're lucky. Hank didn't want no part of that fight but they made him go anyway."

Laurel washed the dishes and tinware, set them out to dry.

"I've got to fetch the eggs and feed the chickens. Just sit comfortable where you like. I won't be long."

She did the chores as quickly as she could, looking toward the cabin every few minutes. When she came back inside, he was in the bedroom. The bureau was bare and the haversack lay beside the door.

"You ain't got need to pack up," Laurel said. "I'll be fixing noon-dinner before long. It'd make me feel a poor host if you just up and left."

For a few moments he didn't tilt his head one way or another.

"It ain't the least bother."

He nodded then.

"You can sit at the table or just rest in here."

He nodded that he'd stay in the bedroom.

Probably tired of my prattling on, Laurel thought, but it had felt so good to speak to someone. She hadn't talked this much since seeing Marcie at the victory jubilee last month. Slidell, good a man as he was, talked easier to Hank than to her. As for Hank, it seemed they spoke a little less each day. Sometimes they'd eat a meal with hardly a word between them. But to never be able to speak, what an awful thing that would be. Music might be the onliest thing that gave you cause to stand it, because it flowed out on your breath like words, and you could hear it. In its way, it answered you.

He's asleep, Laurel thought, but after a while a few notes came from the bedroom and then a song. The whole cabin suddenly became less gloamy, as though the music pulled in more light through the windows and chink gaps. One song blended into another as Laurel got the eggs and milk and flour and mixed the cornbread batter and smoothed it in the bake pan. As she set the table, Laurel wished she knew the songs so she could hum along. She was about to take the cornbread out of the stove when she saw Hank in the doorway listening. Laurel wiped her hands on her apron and went to the door.

"You ever heard anything as pretty?" she asked softly.

"It's nice to the ear," Hank admitted, his voice soft too.

Hank came inside. He stepped lightly across the puncheon floor. Laurel took the cornbread from the stove and quietly closed the metal door. She set the bread basket and yellowware bowl on the table and poured spring water in the cups. Only when the song ended did she go to the bedroom door and tell Walter the meal was ready.

"You look a sight more alive than when we hauled you in," Hank said when Walter joined them. "So you'll be heading on, I guess."

Walter nodded as Laurel passed him the bowl.

"There's plenty so don't be shy about taking what you want. We much admired your music earlier, didn't we, Hank?"

"It was pleasing enough," Hank said.

"That's what you do, play music, to make a living I mean?" Laurel asked.

Walter nodded.

"And you were on your way to New York to play music but something happened?"

Walter nodded again.

"If you'd been robbed you'd not have that sixty dollars," Laurel said, "but whatever happened, it caused you to get lost up here, right?"

Walter nodded.

"I guess I was wrong to take you for a tramp," Hank said, and for the first time Laurel noticed a change in his tone. "There's a lot I'd think you not able to do since you can't talk, but your being able to make your music, people got to respect that."

They spoke little for a few minutes, Walter again taking only food he was offered, something that she could tell Hank noticed too. After they finished, Walter walked over to the bookshelf and pointed at the yellow pencils, waiting until Laurel nodded that it was okay. He came back to the table and took the note from his pocket and turned it over.

"I thought you couldn't read nor write?" Laurel said.

Walter drew two vertical lines, across them six slashes. He studied his drawing a moment and flipped the pencil stem and shortened the slashes with the eraser, brushed off the specks of rubber.

"You want to know where the railroad is?" Hank asked.

Walter nodded.

"It's in Mars Hill," Hank said. "You want to go there so you can get on to New York, I reckon?"

Walter nodded.

"It's a three-mile walk from here," Laura said. "That's likely too far after what you've been through, but Slidell goes every Saturday. He lives up at the notch. He's got a horse and wagon and he'd not mind taking you."

"Maybe Walter don't want to wait till Saturday," Hank said.

"We don't mind you staying on a few days," Laurel said. "You could help Hank stob the fences up, make you some extra money for your trip."

"You think I might have the least little say in this," Hank interrupted.

"He'll lose his way without someone going with him, especially since he can't read nor talk," Laurel said. "Besides, you're the one always says it's shameful that a man of Slidell's years is over here helping most every day. Walter and you could get that fence near raised by Saturday."

"Sister, you don't even know if he's ever done farmwork."

"Ask him then."

"Have you?" Hank asked.

Walter paused, then nodded.

"What about all them stings?" Hank said to Laurel. "A minute ago you was fretting he'd be too puny to walk three miles."

"If he gets to feeling puny he can stop and rest."

Hank looked at her steadily for a few moments, like he saw something he'd not taken much notice of before. He raised his nubbed wrist and showed Walter where the skin had been knit into a crisscross of stitches.

"There's things I can't do by my ownself, so I'll put a dollar a day in your pocket if it proves out you know what you're doing. That'll give you four dollars to add to what you already got, enough for a new shirt and britches, city clothes that fit. Four and a half if you got the grit to start today."

"You can wait till morning," Laurel said, but Walter nodded again and rose from the table.

"I'll get the hammer and nails," Hank said as they walked out the door. "The wire's already up there but I'll need you to fetch some locust posts."

Laurel cleared the table, but before doing anything else she went to the window and peeked out. There'd be women who would fault his sharp-honed features, she knew, but he was handsome in his way. Hank was crossing the pasture, in his hand a pail holding staples and a hammer. Walter stood next to the barn, but he wasn't loading his arms with locust posts. Instead, he looked first at Hank before glancing toward the cabin. He kneeled and slipped something into the rock foundation.

Walter looked around once more and rose, began filling his arms with locust posts.

Laurel waited a few minutes and then took a roundabout way to the barn so the men didn't see her. She felt inside the rock gap and found the chain and medallion. Save his life and take him in and he figures us to steal from him, Laurel thought, and grabbled deeper, expecting to find the money too. Nothing else was hidden. She studied the medallion's one word, whispered how it might be pronounced before placing it back. She went to the cabin and opened the dictionary, thumbed past *T* and *U* before stopping at *V*. Laurel set her index finger on the slick onionskin paper and moved her finger down one page and on to the next. The word wasn't there.

II

CHAPTER SIX

Chauncey rose from his desk and walked to the recruiting office's window. His gaze lifted over Lusk's Barbershop and the post office and up the swath of green grass to the college's clock tower. Fifteen minutes. Most men would pull down the blinds and leave and no one would think the least thing about it, but Chauncey Feith couldn't do that. The one time he had, Ben Lusk lifted his white smock and checked his pocket watch, then looked at Chauncey like he'd just saluted a portrait of Kaiser Wilhelm. He sat back down and lifted the brass paperweight and straightened the recruitment forms, placed the paperweight back on the restacked paper.

Except for breaking up the brawl on the boardwalk, it had

been another slow week. Which was only to be expected. The men who really wanted to fight for their country had volunteered last fall when America entered the fray. Now, with folks believing the war all but won, there was even more excuse not to enlist, though that didn't keep Captain Arnold at regional headquarters from blaming Chauncey when he didn't meet his enlistment quota.

Boyce Clayton passed by the window and Chauncey watched him cross the street and walk down the boardwalk to the Turkey Trot Gentlemen's Club. When the tower's bell rang, Chauncey would go to the Turkey Trot himself and ask about Boyce's nephew Paul. It wasn't something he wanted to do, or had to do for that matter. It would even be after he was officially off duty. Yet he owed it to Paul. Just one more thing that people in Mars Hill hardly noticed, or if they did notice took the wrong way. If folks like Ben Lusk or Marvin Alexander at the post office saw Chauncey entering the Turkey Trot, they'd believe he was only going to get liquored up, not inquire about a wounded soldier.

It was the same with Chauncey getting up fifteen minutes early to spit shine his shoes and iron his uniform. He never left the house until he'd checked that the RS and US on the collar buttons were aligned, the blue hat cord perfectly centered. Doing it just to look spiffy was what people wanted to think, not realizing that when potential recruits came in, especially the farm boys in overalls and brogans, they'd imagine themselves wearing the polished shoes and fresh-pressed uniform. Chauncey saw it in the way the boys scanned him from head to toe, not just inside the recruiting office but when he walked around town or drove out to visit a farm. Even Paul Clayton had once been like that, shyly asking to wear Chauncey's campaign hat so he could look in a mirror with it on. Chauncey had let him.

Later, when Paul turned eighteen, Boyce and his brother Ansel had tried to talk him out of volunteering, telling their nephew that his mother needed him more than the army did.

The bell finally rang and Chauncey closed the blinds. He made a last inspection to ensure he left the office in good order before walking out. As Chauncey turned the key, he saw his face reflected in the window. The skin was smooth and clear, which wasn't always good since the slightest thing made him look flummoxed when he really wasn't. But like his mother said, Chauncey had a strong chin, and people noticed that too. The Turkey Trot was on the outskirts of town so the law and the preachers could pretend it wasn't breaking state law. Veterans drank there, including Tillman Estep, who'd lost an eye and had his face scarred rough as a washboard. The first time he'd seen Estep after his return, Chauncey saluted and Estep didn't return the salute, just glared at Chauncey with his one eye like Chauncey had been the one who sent the mortar round into his trench. Estep went around Mars Hill telling anyone who'd listen that the war was nothing more than a bunch of men killing each other for a few acres of mud. Saying such things hurt morale on the home front, and things were already bad enough. The county was all but overrun with Germans. They spoke German, telling each other who knew what, and ate German food and just because they didn't wear Hun army uniforms no one seemed worried a bit by them being here.

Chauncey walked down the street toward the one-windowed clapboard building. He pushed through the swinging doors, paused a moment to adjust to the lesser light. Tillman Estep sat at the table nearest the entrance, almost like he'd planned it so Chauncey would see him first. A man wearing an overseas cap sat at the table as well. Chauncey didn't know his name, but he'd heard about the man and his ailment. Just pretend you were looking for someone else and leave, Chauncey told himself, but others had noticed him now, including Boyce Clayton, who was at the bar talking to Toby Meachum. Three old men sat on stools at the bar's far end, liquor bottles out in the open. Maybe because of his war veteran clientele, or bribes, Meachum no longer pretended his "Gentlemen's Club" was anything but a saloon. No one looked especially glad to see Chauncey, including Meachum, who began polishing the bar, acting like he hadn't noticed his coming in. Didn't turn away when he needed money from Feith Savings and Loan to buy this building, Chauncey thought.

The air suddenly seemed thicker and his ribs felt like laces pulled tight around his lungs, but Chauncey squared his shoulders and stepped to the bar, remembering his father's advice on his first day at the bank—look confident and people notice and acknowledge that confidence. Chauncey placed his left boot firmly on the brass railing. Boyce, like Tillman Estep and the three old men at the bar end, chased his beer with a shot glass of clear liquid. Moonshine, and it was Boyce and Ansel Clayton who supplied it to Meachum. They probably didn't think Chauncey knew about such things, but it was part of a recruiting officer's job, at least a good one, to know what went on not just in Mars Hill but the whole county, especially since some of the youths in his Boys Working Reserve lived as far north as Shelton Laurel and south to Moody Knob.

Refusing to drink anything other than brown liquor was the sign of good breeding. That was something else his father had taught him, but there were times like this when doing so would seem high nosed and putting on airs. At the bank Chauncey had always known how to show customers he thought himself no better than anyone else. Sometimes it was using phrases like "lipping full" or "just as lief," or offering his hand first to shake, yes sirring a farmer who owned nothing more than a couple of acres and a swaybacked mule, or rising from his chair when some snuff-gummed widow came in with her coupon book.

"I'll have the same as Boyce here, Meachum," Chauncey said, smacking a half eagle on the varnished wood, "and a round for all at the bar. Whatever they want, and pour yourself one. We're drinking to Paul Clayton, a true hero."

The old men offered slurred thank yous and tapped their shot glasses for Meachum to fill. The bartender drew Chauncey's beer and set it on the counter with a shot glass. He poured the moonshine, then went down the bar and filled the old men's glasses.

"Have you another beer, Boyce," Chauncey said, "long as it ain't Schlitz or some other Hun beer Meachum's hiding back there."

"I'm fine," Boyce answered.

"Pour yourself one, Meachum," Chauncey said.

The bartender hesitated, then drew himself a beer and picked up the gold piece. The cash register chimed and the wooden drawer slid open. Meachum returned with four silver dollars, stacked them on the bar like poker chips.

Chauncey raised his shot glass and the old drunks did as well. He looked at Meachum and the bartender raised his tankard.

"To Paul Clayton, a hero," Chauncey said.

He knew they were watching to see if he'd sip like a nancy pants or drink like a man. Chauncey tilted the glass and swallowed as if the shine was nothing more than a shot of sarsaparilla. It went down easier than he'd expected, an oily warmth settling in his stomach. He held the empty shot glass aloft for all to see, then set it down hard enough that the glass rang against the wood.

A chair scratched and Chauncey looked in the mirror. The man with Estep muttered something and stood, his hand still on his stomach. Tillman Estep helped the man to the entrance, a brief unfolding of late-afternoon light as the doors swung. The man had come back from Europe convinced, though he'd had no wound, that his guts were torn up. A doctor in Asheville said it was because he'd bayoneted a German. Chauncey knew such things happened, had read about it in a pamphlet the army sent him. Sometimes snipers went blind or a man who'd shot another in the leg would become lame. Still, any shirker could playact such a thing to get out of the war.

Chauncey began to feel the alcohol. Nothing much, just a soft buzzing in the back of his brain. He'd heard moonshine was twice as potent as bourbon, but he'd once drunk half a bottle of L & G and never slurred a word.

"What do you hear about your nephew?" Chauncey asked. "They still think Paul to be up there awhile?"

"Three more months," Boyce said, staring at his glass as he spoke.

Chauncey took a swallow of his beer and tapped his shot glass against the bar. Meachum came over and refilled it.

"That's some fine white liquor you're pouring," Chauncey said. "When those doctors in Washington are done, all Paul will need is a couple of glasses of this and he'll be totally cured."

"That's God's own truth," one of the old men said as Chauncey drained his shot glass. "It'll cure most any ailings a fellow can have."

Chauncey swallowed and set the glass down hard again as the alcohol made its slow slide into his stomach.

"Yes, that's quality whiskey," Chauncey said, and winked at Meachum. "Whoever made it knew what he was doing. Right, Boyce?"

"I'd not know," Boyce answered.

"Of course not," Chauncey said and grinned. "There couldn't be anybody in these parts running a still. It's probably something those Canucks brewed."

Boyce emptied his shot glass and took a long swallow of beer. Chauncey felt his face starting to tingle. It wasn't an unpleasant sensation, more like drizzle on a hot summer day. An amber glow now limned the room. He looked at his reflection in the mirror, let his eyes settle on the sergeant's stripes. Estep and the other man had been privates, both sent home after six months, but Chauncey had been in the army ten months already and was still in. His eyes drifted from his own face to Estep's. At a district meeting, Captain Arnold had said there were men so afraid before battle that their nipples gave milk. So cowardly they were trying to turn themselves into women, Captain Arnold claimed. For all Chauncey knew, Estep could have been chicken enough to do that. It wouldn't surprise him a bit.

Boyce finished the beer and stepped from the bar.

"You tell Paul we'll do something special for him when he gets back home," Chauncey said.

Boyce gave the slightest nod and walked out.

"We will," Chauncey said, and one of the old men grunted in assent.

He could leave now too, but Chauncey didn't feel like leaving anymore, at least not yet. Five months he'd avoided Estep, sometimes crossing the street so as not to pass him. People had noticed. He knew they'd rather believe Chauncey did it out of fear than out of contempt for a man who had to be conscripted to fight, the same as they'd rather believe he had gotten to be a recruiter because his father and Senator Zeller knew each other. Captain Arnold himself had told Chauncey the day of his commission that if Chauncey Feith wasn't the right man for the job he wouldn't have appointed him even if his father was Woodrow Wilson.

Chauncey studied the mirrored face he'd avoided too long, looking at every inch, the ridged scars and even the sunk flesh where Estep's eye had been. Meachum polished the bar near the old men, rubbing the same spot over and over like it was a magic lamp he hoped to summon a genie from. Probably wishing I'd leave, Chauncey thought, and tapped the glass, not so much for a drink as to make Meachum quit pretending he wasn't in the room. Meachum brought over the bottle.

"You sure?" the bartender asked, saying it soft, but not soft enough that the others couldn't hear.

The old men gandered his way. Estep looked up as well.

"I wouldn't ask for it if I didn't want it," Chauncey said. "Pour my damn drink."

He lifted the glass and drained it and looked around. The liquor didn't settle as easy this time.

"That's some fierce drinking you're doing there," one of the old men said, and raised his empty shot glass. "I'd toast you if I had me some more nectar to sup."

"Give him another, Meachum," Chauncey said, and Meachum poured the man a drink.

"To you, sir," the man said, raising the glass, "and all men like you what have worn the uniform."

A scoff came from the back of the room. Don't give him the pleasure of acknowledging it, Chauncey told himself. The old men hadn't seemed to notice, Meachum either, who was back polishing the bar. But it didn't matter if they had heard because Chauncey Feith didn't give a damn what Estep or any of the rest of them thought, and that included Hank Shelton and his smart-ass remark when all Chauncey had done was remind Shelton and the rest of them who the real enemy was. He thought about Estep, who could laze all day in a saloon and no one said a word about it, but if Chauncey left his office fifteen minutes early the same folks went into conniptions.

The liquor began to sour in his stomach. Rotgut, that's what some called it, and with good reason. As Chauncey stared in the mirror, he thought how a soldier in Europe could be a fool or a coward for months and act brave one time, maybe for just a few seconds, and everything he'd done wrong was forgotten. Or maybe not even brave for a few seconds. From what Chauncey knew, all Estep had done was stand in a trench, probably cowering there because he was too chickenshit to leave it. The same was true of Hank Shelton. Some folks would think him quite the fellow because he tried to take water to a wounded soldier. They'd forget all about the cove and that witchy sister of his. But Shelton himself admitted he'd thought it was a Tommy since the man called for water in English. He'd probably figured there wasn't a Hun within miles. Shelton hadn't gone alone either. Another American soldier went with him and he got the worst of it, shot in the chest and nearly dying. If Hank Shelton had known it was a German sniper, or that one was close by, he'd probably have been afraid to go. Yet they'd both been given purple hearts, like Shelton and Estep had done nothing but be heroes the whole time. And now they got to come back and act like Chauncey Feith wasn't near the man they were, even mock his first name, too ignorant to know that the name Chauncey meant chancellor, a leader.

What Chauncey did took courage too. It wasn't the kind where you had a scar or ribbon you could show off, but instead a day-to-day courage as you stood up for what you believed no matter what. An unsung hero, because you couldn't go around telling people that any man could hold a rifle and stand in a trench but only a select few could do what a general or commodore or recruiter did. Regular soldiers needed to believe they were the ones who mattered most, and that's what Chauncey did with every recruit. He made each one feel special and he never forgot for a single moment that a few of them would be special, real heroes like Paul Clayton, who'd wiped out two Hun machine-gun nests and won a Silver Star.

Another of the old men raised his empty glass.

"I'd like to toast you as well, sir, except I've got nary a drop."

Chauncey pushed another silver dollar in Meachum's direction and the bartender filled the glass.

"I'm glad to buy any man in this room a drink as long as he's not a shirker," Chauncey said loudly.

"To you and the uniform," the old drunk slurred.

"Who are you calling a shirker, Feith?" Estep asked.

The old men quit talking and Meachum stopped wiping the bar.

"I said, who you calling a shirker, Feith?"

He watched in the mirror as Estep pushed back his chair and stood.

"I'm not talking about you," Chauncey said.

"Who are you talking about then," Estep asked, "besides yourself?"

Meachum came around the bar and stood in front of Estep.

"This doesn't concern you, Meachum," Estep said.

"It does if it's happening here," Meachum answered.

For a few moments no one spoke.

"Yeah, I guess it does, especially since the savings and loan's got a note on you," Estep said.

The veteran turned and shoved through the swinging doors, so late in the day now that no light flashed in from outside. Meachum returned to the bar with the table's empty glasses. He doused them in a bucket of gray water and wiped each one dry before setting it on a cloth.

"Estep knew I wasn't talking about him," Chauncey said.

Meachum didn't turn around. Chauncey picked up his change and turned to leave, but the room tilted and he grabbed the bar edge. Give yourself a minute, he told himself. Chauncey tried to recall why he'd come into the Turkey Trot in the first place and remembered. He thought about how Paul Clayton hadn't waited to be conscripted but had come into the recruiting office on his eighteenth birthday and volunteered despite his mother and uncles telling him not to. When Paul had finished signing the forms, the first thing he did was salute Chauncey. It had been all he could do not to shed a tear, especially since Paul had been one of the first to join Chauncey's chapter of the Boys Working Reserve.

He slowly crossed the floor and passed through the doors. If he went home soused, his father would be displeased and his mother would cry, so Chauncey decided to go to the recruiting office instead. After a few stabs at the key hole, he got inside and turned on the electric light. The black letters on the eye chart bobbed a few moments before resettling in their proper positions. Chauncey sat down at his desk and placed his brow on his forearms as the nausea came again. He tried to be perfectly still, his breaths mere sips of air that went no farther than the top of his lungs. He imagined his insides a froth of foul water that had to be calmed. It helped and he began to feel better.

He opened the desk's bottom drawer and took out his speech for the next jubilee. It was a bully speech, one the governor of North Carolina himself would be proud to give. Which was no surprise because Chauncey had always been good with words. At the bank, he'd been able to sit down with men three times his age and convince them that their money was better off in Feith Savings and Loan than hidden in a tin can, or explain why a mortgage was the best way to secure a loan. Chauncey had always found the words to assuage their concerns, just as he did now with parents and wives and sometimes the recruits themselves.

The tower bell chimed eight times before Chauncey felt sober enough to go home. A headache was forming like a thundercloud, but before it erupted an idea came to him. He'd show Estep and Meachum and every other person in Mars Hill that Sergeant Chauncey Feith could lead by example as well as words. He'd show them he could lead not just a troop of boys but a whole community. When Paul Clayton got out of the hospital, he'd have the best homecoming of any soldier in the whole state.

CHAPTER SEVEN

Wednesday morning after the men went to the pasture, Laurel stood before the books on the makeshift shelf. She ran her index finger down each one. Keep reading and studying them, Miss Calicut had told her that long-ago September when school started again, that way you can stay caught up until enough parents realize how silly they're acting. By then your father may be sprier too. Even with all the meanness she had endured from other pupils, Miss Calicut had made school the best place Laurel had ever known. Everywhere in the classroom there was something special—on the back wall a map of the United States and around it pictures of a beach in Florida with white sand and a blue ocean, a field of purple wildflowers in Nebraska, another of buildings in New York so tall they were called skyscrapers, another of an orange canyon in Texas. There'd been a globe in the room and Laurel could spin it and the whole world pass before her, each continent a different color. Miss Calicut had a big table next to her desk too, and on it were boxes with pretty rocks and a glass case with butterflies and moths. Real American and North Carolina flags stood by the doorway and beside them a shelf you could pick a book from to borrow over a weekend. Even now, sixteen years later, Laurel had seen more of the world in that one classroom than anywhere outside it.

Miss Calicut had been young and pretty and she knew all sorts of interesting things about different places, like what people wore and ate, and if the country had mountains or deserts and what kinds of animals lived there. When Miss Calicut read books aloud like *Anne of Green Gables* and *Great Expectations*, she changed her voice for the different people in the book and it seemed you knew those people in the realest sort of way. Miss Calicut was always bringing in a plant or bug and once even a live snake and she'd feature something about it that you didn't know. Best of all, she made Laurel feel different in a good way, doing small things like hugging her every morning or letting her take the roll or ring the recess bell. One time when a town girl teased about her homespun dress, Miss Calicut told Laurel that the other girl was jealous because her own mother couldn't sew. Whenever she made the highest test grade or won a spell down, Miss Calicut bragged on her and said Laurel had the smarts to be a tip-top schoolteacher, said it in front of the whole class. On that last day, Miss Calicut had given her the seventh-grade textbooks and a brand-new dictionary. *For Laurel Shelton, with great expectations for one of my favorite students*, Miss Calicut had written on the dictionary's first page. She'd hugged Laurel and said that as bad as things were they'd get better. It will be good teacher practice for you, Miss Calicut told her, you'll be your own pupil. Laurel had studied the books all that fall, working out the ciphering, reading, even making up tests for herself. She'd taught Hank some too, though he soon lost interest. But her father had got more needsome every day and by the new year all the books were skiffed with dust.

Laurel lifted her finger from the last book, wiped the dust on her dress. She took the apron and pan off their pegs and the sack of green beans from the alcove. Once on the porch, she sat in a chair with the sack beside her and the pan at her feet. Laurel watched the men work as she snapped beans and tossed them in the pan. Walter had done this kind of work before. She heard it in the quick clap of the hammer strikes and the way Hank wasn't stopping to show him how things were done. Surprising considering his smooth hands, his making a living with the flute.

As Laurel set another handful of beans in her lap, she thought about Walter not hiding the sixty dollars. Even if it was gold, the chain and medallion wouldn't up-scale a quarter eagle, and why not hide the flute? A man with lots of swivels to him. He hid one thing but not another, gaumy as any boxcar tramp but with money and silver and gold, couldn't talk or read or write but played the flute so pretty your heart near busted from the wonder of it, a man who made notice of a single green feather. All Laurel knew certain was that she wanted to know more about him and was glad he hadn't left.

He brightens up my life. That's what Marcie said about Robbie, and that was what Walter did. But brightness never stayed long here. Laurel had learned the true of that as a child. The parakeets had flown over the cove like a dense green cloud, but they'd never paused in their passing, never circled or landed. Instead, the birds went over the cove the same way they would a deep murky pond. But one time it was full noon, the few minutes when enough light sifted in for the parakeets to see the orchard and its shriveled fruit. The flock curved back, low enough that Laurel could hear them calling *we we we* as they bunched above the orchard and began swirling downward. One by one, the birds sleeved the orchard limbs in green and orange and yellow. Laurel had been in the cornfield with Hank. She should have run into the orchard right then and chased them away, but she'd just stood watching as two dozen birds pecked and hopped and preened among the branches. It was like their bodies had knit together and lifted the whole cove skyward into the sun's full light.

When her mother saw the parakeets, she'd run to the cabin. Laurel's father had hobbled onto the porch shirtless and barefoot, shotgun in hand, swearing he'd not allow what paltry fruit they had to be taken. Her father had moved unsteadily into the pasture, Laurel's mother beside him with a hay fork. Laurel tried to speak, but no words came. It was Hank who spoke.

"Just scare them away, Daddy."

That was what Laurel thought would happen, because the shotgun wavered in his thin arms. When it went off, the flock bloomed upward. But one bird had been hit, and though it rose too, it quickly lost what grasp it had on the sky. The parakeet landed in the orchard, the hurt wing dragging on the ground. The other birds at first flew west toward the ridge, then turned as one, made a wide arc, and came back, twice flying over the wounded bird before descending. Her father fired again and this time four parakeets fell from the branches. The unharmed birds did not flee as far this time. The bitter smell of cordite filled the orchard as another shot cracked the air and only five parakeets rose. Her mother walked beneath the limbs, gigging wounded birds with the hay fork. When Laurel had run into the orchard and begged her father not to shoot any more, her mother seized her by the arm and said it had to be done. There'd been one more shot before her mother opened the gate and prodded the hogs toward the orchard. They grunted and squealed with each jab, moving forward, slow and contrary, until they saw. The following winter her father placed the barrel between the largest hog's eyes and squeezed the shotgun's trigger. Laurel had refused to eat the sausage and ham, but her mother put the bones in soup, the fatback in beans and cornbread. No matter how little, she could always taste it.

Laurel lifted another handful of beans into her lap and wondered where Walter had found his green feather. She thought about the medallion and the possibility it was a gift from a sweetheart. Not likely. It didn't seem a girl's name or have an etching of a heart on it. Not being able to talk would be a lacking many women couldn't abide, the same way it'd been with Hank's hand, but Laurel could abide it. Hank had to set store by how good a worker Walter was, and there'd be plenty to do before cold weather came, especially if Hank wanted to finish the well. She bet he was already wishing Walter would stay, perhaps starting to feel like Walter could become his friend. Laurel let herself fancy Walter staying another week and another week after that. Maybe the cardinal flower's love potion might really work. If Walter stayed on there might come a time they'd be alone and he'd lean over and buss her on the cheek and after that, as the days went on, the kisses would get longer and she'd start picking the Queen Anne's lace to make a tonic or even the virgin's bower to twine in her hair.

Laurel smiled at her own silliness. It was like years ago when she'd open the wish book and place her finger on this or that, making believe it was something she could actually have. He'll be gone come Saturday, Laurel told herself, and you'll never see him again.

The pan was almost full when she saw Slidell coming out of the woods. Laurel brushed bean strings off her apron and walked out in the yard to meet him.

"Finally found you a hired man, I see," Slidell said as he looped the reins around a dogwood tree.

The hammering had stopped and Hank and Walter were walking toward the cabin.

"For a little while at least."

"Who is he?"

"Walter Smith is his name," Laurel said.

"From around here?"

"No," Laurel said, "New York."

Hank and Walter came into the yard.

"This is Slidell," Hank said to Walter. "He's the fellow who lives up at the notch."

"Good to meet you," Slidell said, and held out his hand.

The two men shook hands.

"His name's Walter," Hank said. "But he can say it out loud no more than that scarecrow yonder can."

"Not being able to talk could be a hard thing," Slidell said, "but I misdoubt there's a man alive who'd not have wished for it sometime in his life, whether saying I do or I'll have one more."

Slidell gestured toward the fence.

"He looks to swing a hammer true enough."

"He does that," Hank agreed. "Only problem is I just got him through Friday. Walter's of a mind to catch a train to New

York. He may be wanting a ride into town with you Saturday."

"That's fine," Slidell said to Walter. "Just be up at the trail notch by full light."

Slidell nodded at the windlass.

"Too bad he's leaving so soon. You might could get that well done before the snow flies."

"What you figure before I sound some water?" Hank asked.

"For you and him together it'd be a full week's work," Slidell said, "lest you get lucky and hit no rock."

"It would be good to get that done," Laurel said.

Hank's face darkened.

"We best stick to getting the fence up. From what I've seen luck don't wander this cove much, excepting the kind nobody wants."

Maybe that's changing, Laurel almost said, but decided saying so might jinx it.

"New York City," Slidell said to Walter. "I'd not have reckoned a big need for wire stringing there, other than they got so many folks they need to keep them from herding off into the ocean."

"He's a musician," Hank said, "and he can play a flute like nobody's business."

"Can he now?" Slidell said. "I'd like to hear that. Bring him to the house tomorrow evening and we'll see if that flute can whistle out some mountain tunes. Ansel and Boyce are fetching me my tonic, and Boyce always brings his dulcimer."

"That tonic ups the ante for coming," Hank said.

"You're not averse to a drink of homemade corn whiskey, are you?" Slidell asked Walter.

"You'll not want to leave these hills without sampling what Ansel and Boyce potion up," Hank said. "It goes down smooth as mama's milk. You'll hardly know you're drunk until your legs numb out on you."

"I've had no better, taxed and sealed included, and I've tested plenty of both," Slidell said. "So I can expect you all?"

"Let us see if we've got enough briskness to. We've not slacked our reins all afternoon and tomorrow we'll make a full day of it. If we don't get up there though, ask Ansel and Boyce how Paul's faring."

Walter nodded toward the posts next to the shed.

"Yeah, we'll need more of them," Hank said. "You go on ahead. I'll be up there in a minute."

"His hands are blistered," Laurel said. "Let me put some salve and a wrap on them first."

Laurel motioned for Walter to come inside. She sat him at the table and took the salve and a hank of cloth from the shelf. She took his hand in hers and tended to the blisters. Hank and Slidell were still out in the yard. Their voices were softer but she could hear them through the open door.

"Anyway," Slidell said. "That fellow you've been trying to impress was up at the notch earlier."

"I thought I saw him there," Hank replied. "By himself?"

"Yeah. I told him he could ride down with me for a better look but he wouldn't." Slidell shook his head. "You'd think a man like Weatherbee wouldn't abide such silly notions."

"More do than don't," Hank replied. "He say anything else?"

"He said you'd fixed up this farm better than he'd have thought you could, so I'd say you've passed your audition."

For a few moments neither man spoke. Laurel finished knotting the cloth on the back of Walter's hand.

"You told her the truth of all this fixing up yet?" Slidell asked.

"The time ain't been right," Hank said.

The men, still talking, walked over to the horse, but Laurel could no longer hear them. Laurel let go of Walter's hand, and they walked onto the porch.

"I'll see you Thursday if not before," Slidell said as he rode out of the yard. "You come too, Laurel."

"That man's been through some hard times in his life," Hank told Walter once Slidell disappeared into the woods. "For you northern folk it was natural to wear the blue in the Confederate War. Slidell's daddy was a Lincolnite too, but it wasn't so common a thing in these mountains. One day three fellows come up from Marshall, outliers but wearing butternut so they could alibi their meanness. Slidell's older brother and daddy was in the field. Those men rode right into that field and shot them dead, even with Slidell's brother but fourteen years old. Slidell was in the barn helping his momma, so him and her hid in the loft. After those bastards stole what they could from the house, they come to the barn. They led the cow and draft horse out. The man trailing had a match. Slidell says he didn't see that match struck but heard the rasping of it. That outlier was about to drop the match when one of the others said don't because he'd be coming back with a wagon for the hay. Slidell and his momma had to do the burying themselves. There was a shotgun hid under a mattress and Slidell got it out. Twelve years old but he'd have gone after them except for his momma begging him not to leave her to fend alone. If she hadn't, that hand of cards would have been played out full. He did go looking for them after the war, but they'd run off like cur dogs to Texas. Slidell says he'll never forget the sound of that match being struck and that barn so stoked with dry hay it'd have gone up like a rag doused with kerosene. I don't notion I'd ever forget hearing that match strike neither."

Hank nodded at the locust posts.

"Bring up a load with you and we'll get back to it."

Walter nodded and the men left the yard. Laurel finished with the beans and then went into the field to hoe the corn. She worked barefoot, her feet and ankles soon darkened by the loosened soil. She'd tied her hair back, and as she paused at a row end she straightened and looked up at the pasture.

Hank set the wire in the crowbar's claw and pulled against the brace while Walter pounded the staples and used the tamping rod to unroll the wire. When the tone of the metal staple entering the fourth post deepened, Hank moved to the next end post, set his left knee against the wood, and pulled downward with the crowbar until the wire was taut. When they braced the fence, Hank didn't check that Walter blunted the nails so as not to split the lentle. Trusting him already to do things right.

Trusting everyone but her, Laurel couldn't help thinking. From what Hank had said to Slidell, he hadn't told Carolyn, at least not an out-and-out proposal, that he was ready to marry. Yet most everyone else, including Carolyn's daddy, seemed to know. At least that was one thing she and Carolyn shared. Laurel looked up at the notch. Last week she'd seen Carolyn's father up there herself. An audition, Slidell had called it. Be glad he passed it, Laurel told herself. It just means they'll get married sooner, and you and Carolyn can start getting used to each other and become friends. Her being down here, it'll finally show folks there can be some happiness in this cove.

CHAPTER EIGHT

When Laurel's mother died, her father had covered the mirror and let the Franklin clock run down so he could still the hands on the ten and the two, mark the death time. Two months passed before he rewound the metal key. But the hands had been locked in one place so long they seemed unable to free themselves, and so remained on the ten and two. Last winter, the days had been so long Laurel would look at the clock and almost believe it was still running, that time had slowed so much a minute could feel like a day. But now that she wanted time to slow down, it passed faster than any time in her life. Already it was Thursday evening. One more day and one more night and he'd be gone.

"Glad we got that upper pasture almost done," Hank said, "for it looks likely to rain tomorrow."

They were on the porch, Hank perched on the railing while Walter and Laurel sat beside each other in the ladderback chairs. Walter's eyes were closed. He'd worked hard all week, enough to have Hank say that with Walter's help for a couple more months the farm would be in tip-top shape. But Laurel knew she'd miss Walter more than Hank would, even though she still knew little about him. He'd raised two fingers when she asked if he had any sisters and no fingers when she asked about brothers, five when she asked how many years he'd worked as a musician. She'd found out a few other things but not near as much as she wanted to. If only one person could ask questions, after a while it sounded like you were being nosy. Some things he couldn't answer anyway. When Laurel asked how he'd gotten to the cove he'd simply shrugged. When she asked where he'd found the green feather, he nodded toward the ridge where she'd found him. On this side? she asked, but he shook his head.

But just sitting beside him at the table and on the porch had been nice. She was used to not talking, she could stand that well enough. It was not having someone to share the silence, the way it had been last winter, that was the terrible thing. Laurel wondered if Walter understood that about her, that she was as used to silence as he was. She wondered how he had managed in New York. Did he point at what he wanted to buy, unlatch his door to anyone who knocked? And not being able to read and write. What if he needed to buy something that he couldn't point to, or needed directions to a place?

"Are you too frazzled to go up to Slidell's and sip whiskey, Walter?" Hank asked.

Walter opened his eyes and nodded.

"Yeah, I'm beat too," Hank said, "though I'd deeply enjoy some of the Clayton boys' lumbago draught."

"It would be good to know how Paul's doing," Laurel said, and turned to Walter. "That's Ansel and Boyce's nephew. He got hurt bad in the war."

They sat in silence a few minutes, the light diminishing, appearing not so much to drain from the sky as to seep into the cove's dark floor. Up in the trees, jarflies started droning. A breeze came up and Laurel smelled a dampness in it.

"New York," Hank said. "Is that where you lived all your life?"

Walter nodded.

"But you couldn't have lived there your whole life, not and know how to raise a fence like you do."

"You mean New York State?" Laurel asked.

When Walter didn't reply, Laurel went inside and fetched *Frye's Grammar School Geography*. She moved her chair closer so that the pages spilled onto both their laps, their forearms touching as she balanced the book between them. She felt the gold hairs on Walter's arm, the warmth of his skin. She found a map of New York State.

"Show me."

Walter pointed north of the city where the black dots and the names beneath them were sparse.

"Near Ithaca?" Laurel asked.

Walter nodded.

"So you left there to go to New York City," Hank asked, "to play music, I mean?"

"It's no wonder, good as you are," Laurel said when Walter nodded. "I still can't figure out how you ended up here though. It had to be some adventure."

"I'd like to hear that story too," Hank agreed. "I bet it'd fill a book big as the one Laurel's holding."

The jarflies continued their racket in the trees. An owl near the barn hooted, was answered from somewhere in the deeper woods. Then other voices, human voices. Slidell emerged from the woods on Ginny, behind him two other men on horseback. At first Laurel couldn't tell who they were, then saw the high foreheads and broad shoulders, red hair tinged with gray. Slidell had his guitar case strapped to his saddle. What the two brothers brought with them was more curious. Balanced on Boyce's lap was an oblong wooden box shaped like a child's casket. Ansel wore a feed sack around his neck, a thin rope sewn through its top for a drawstring. A pair of bulging black eyes poked out of the sack. As the men got closer, Laurel saw the eyes belonged to a small bat-eared dog. The three men tethered their horses and dismounted. Ansel took the sack off his neck and laid it gently on the ground. As the dog wiggled free of the cloth, Laurel saw Ansel dip a hand in his pocket and withdraw something pinched between forefinger and thumb. He made a quick crossing motion over his heart and rubbed his hand on his shirt. Salt, Laurel knew, and knew the wherefore of his doing it. Like they're afraid I might forget what folks think of me, Laurel thought.

"You can't leave without I have you meet Ansel and Boyce," Hank said when Walter rose to go inside.

"That's right," Slidell said, "especially since I told these boys Hank's got a crackerjack fife player down here, all the way from New York at that."

Slidell freed the battered guitar case from his side saddle. Boyce tucked the box under an arm and used his free hand to remove a corked jug from the saddle bag. Ansel unwrapped a meaty hog bone and laid it before the dog.

"Figured if you wouldn't come to us, we'd come to you," Slidell said. "Share some good whiskey, maybe some tolerable music."

"I can be persuaded to the whiskey part," Hank said, "but you'll have to ask Walter if he'll lip that flute for you."

Walter looked unsure but finally nodded.

"You know Slidell," Hank said to Walter. "That one with the Santy Claus beard is Ansel and the other's Boyce. Come on up on the porch, gentlemen. Walter ain't no revenue man and even if he was he couldn't tell on you."

"I confidenced them of that," Slidell said, smiling. "They've been of a wary nature since their scare last week."

The men ascended the steps. Laurel offered to bring out more chairs but only Slidell accepted. Ansel sat on the railing beside Hank. Boyce squatted in the corner, the oblong box set before him. He uncorked the jug and passed it to Hank, who drank and offered the whiskey to Walter.

"You'll never taste any that beads up better and it's smooth as freestone water," Hank said.

Walter took a tentative sip and passed the jug to Slidell.

"That fyce of yours looks to be living the high life," Hank said to Ansel. "Prime hog meat and rides in the saddle."

"That dog earned it," Slidell said. "You want to tell it, Ansel, or you want me to?"

"Go ahead," Ansel said. "I done talked it out one time today."

"These boys was running their copper above Ansel's place. Just finished bottling a full run when they heard hounds coming up the creek, the revenue man and the high sheriff right behind. There wasn't near enough time to hide everything, so Ansel leaves Boyce to haul the still and jars into a thicket whilst he takes that fyce yonder and gets a ways down the creek, staying in the water all the while. Ansel takes off his shirt and ties it around that fyce's neck and says "get home" and that dog takes off like Caesar's ghost, dragging the shirt through mud holes and briars all the while. He kept it on though."

Slidell stopped and turned to Ansel.

"That's right, ain't it, it being on him the whole way?"

"I took that shirt off him my ownself," Ansel answered. "He did seem to find every briar to run it through and that shirt's the worse for the trip, but I'd rather be wearing an old shirt with tears than a new one with black-and-white stripes."

"They followed the fyce?" Hank asked.

"Damn right," Slidell said. "Led them dogs and them following right back to Ansel's cabin. The high sheriff and the revenue man was so flummoxed they didn't bother going back up the creek. Just called it a day and went home."

"That must have been a sight in the world to see," Hank said. "I'd have paid admission to watch that show."

"Anyway, what you're drinking now, you can thank that fyce for it," Slidell said, "so I'd treat him with some respect."

"Next time I'm in town I'll buy him a prime ham bone myself for that good deed," Hank said.

The men passed the jug, Hank raising it to toast the dog. When the whiskey was offered to Walter again he declined. Hank didn't offer it to Laurel. He wouldn't, she knew, but not because she wasn't a man. Afraid if he did, Boyce and Ansel wouldn't drink from it. Yet they'd drink after Hank, not even rubbing a sleeve over the jug's mouth before they did.

"I got muscadine wine in the larder," Laurel said to Walter. "You'd be better off drinking it than what's festering in that jug, especially come morning."

She went inside and got the bottle and two tin cups. She poured some in a cup and swallowed, tasted the deep purple of the muscadines. Laurel handed the cup to Walter.

"Taste of it," she said.

He sipped from the cup and nodded.

"You go ahead and drink that," Laurel said, and poured herself half a cup.

She took another swallow and felt the wine dribble down her throat.

"Anybody else want some?" Laurel asked, but all the men, including Hank, shook their heads.

"But you haven't tried this, Hank," she said, and offered him the cup. "I made it last September while you were gone."

"I'm fine with what's in that jug," Hank answered.

"Just a taste," Laurel said, still holding the cup out.

"No," Hank said firmly, looking away.

How long will it be before you'll let me and Carolyn drink from the same dipper, Laurel was tempted to ask.

Hank turned to Ansel.

"What do you hear about Paul?"

"The telegram said his lungs is scorched. Hurt his eyes too but he ain't blinded, and that's a blessing for there's many what have been. But he won't never be the man he was. That's some sorry bastards to use gas like that."

"Even in a war, you'd think some things wouldn't be allowed," Boyce added.

"Yes, you'd think so," Slidell said, then more softly, "but it never seems the way of it. Hank knows that as much as I do."

"No, what happened to you was worse," Hank said. "I was a soldier, not a child."

For a few moments the men were quiet. Walter had finished

the wine but shook his head when Laurel offered more. She finished her cup and set it beside the bottle as well.

"They say for sure yet when Paul's coming home?" Slidell asked.

"He'll be in that Washington hospital till November," Ansel said. "If he's doing okay then, they'll send him home."

"Feith's talking up a big to-do when Paul's train comes in," Boyce added, "having a band and letting the schoolkids come and all such doings."

"I bet Miss Calicut will have her class go," Laurel said.

"She best not for their sake," Hank said. "Feith is liable to sign them up."

"That's the God's truth," Ansel agreed. "He's a gung-ho fellow for getting a body volunteered and over to the fight."

"Except if that fellow is his ownself," Hank said.

"Having a rich daddy does have advantages when a war starts up," Boyce said. "Get to put on a uniform and no one within a thousand miles who'll kill you for the wearing of it."

"He still got those school lads dandied up in shirts and britches?" Hank asked.

"He was last Saturday," Boyce said. "Feith struts them around like peacocks, all the while them saluting and yes sirring him. Gives him something to do when he's not bedeviling that German professor."

"Feith claims him for a Hun sympathizer, maybe even a spy," Ansel added. "Yes, sir, Sergeant Feith and his troops will be storming that college any day now, dodging chalk and erasers all the while."

"Makes me and Ansel glad we don't get to town much," Boyce said. "It's bad enough to hear about such nonsense, much less see it."

Slidell lifted his guitar from the case and leaned close to the instrument. He plucked each string and then turned the wooden pegs until he was satisfied.

"Fetch out your dulcimer, Boyce," Slidell said, and turned to Hank. "These boys said they can't stay long."

Boyce opened the case and settled the dulcimer on his lap, a raven feather in his right hand. Walter was looking at the dulcimer intently.

"You ever played one of those?" Laurel asked.

Walter shook his head.

"But you've heard one before?"

Walter nodded.

Slidell and Boyce began to play and Ansel joined in. As Ansel sang *And there's no sickness, toil, or danger in that bright world to which we go,* Laurel wondered if Walter believed what the song claimed, that there was a place where no one got sick and the lame walked and he would be able to speak. But what good did that do in the here and now. It gave you some hope, Laurel supposed, and that was something, but it didn't change the day to day very much.

"That was a good one," Hank said as the men paused and passed the jug.

"Amazing how a couple of drinks always makes my guitar sound better," Slidell said. "I guess some of the fumes seep into the wood and oil the squeaks out of it."

Slidell turned to Walter.

"Get that fife of yours and join us."

Walter hesitated.

"I'll fetch it for you," Laurel told him, and went inside.

"I've not seen a fife like that one," Slidell said when she returned with the flute. "Mind if I have a gander?"

She handed it to him. Slidell let the flute balance in his palm, measuring the weight as he read the words etched on it. Slidell whistled softly and handed the flute back.

"Pure silver and made in Paris. Good thing it was there instead of Vienna. If it had been, Sergeant Feith would claim you're bunging spy notes in it."

The men began "Shady Grove." Walter listened to the first verse and then raised the flute to his mouth. He entered the song so smoothly that Laurel wouldn't have known he was playing except his fingers moved and lips rounded. It wasn't so much a soaring sound but something on the song's surface, like a water strider crossing a creek pool.

"You two are going down a trail I can't follow," Boyce soon said, and raised his hands palms up as if surrendering.

Ansel quit singing as Walter and Slidell played on. The guitar and flute tightly wove their sounds and then untangled them, did that several times until Slidell shook his head and the guitar's strings stilled. Walter played on for a few more notes. When it was over, the only sound was the fyce grinding the bone.

"That's the damndest thing I ever heard," Boyce finally said. "It makes me want to turn this dulcimer into a ball swatter."

"You two ought to haul that down to Asheville," Ansel added. "They's folks will pay cash money for music handsome as that."

"There's a blessingness in the having heard it," Laurel said, touching Walter's forearm and leaving it there for a few moments.

"More Walter than me," Slidell said. "I was the caboose dragged along by the engine."

They played on, Slidell drinking alone now.

"Be careful, Slidell," Hank warned. "That stuff's going to light up your head like a stick of dynamite."

"It's same as snake poison," Slidell replied. "Keep getting bit and it don't hurt you near as bad."

Darkness filled the cove now but for the lantern's yellow smudge. Boyce looked toward the notch and laid the dulcimer back in its case.

"Time to go," he said to his brother, who nodded and stood.

"Just a couple more songs," Slidell said, but the brothers stepped off the porch.

Slidell put up his guitar and rose as well, wavering as he stood. He lifted the jug, tilted it but nothing sloshed.

"Ah, me," Slidell sighed. "Nary a thing left but a skullbuster come morning."

The three men mounted their horses and went up the trail, the lantern's glow quickly vanishing.

"Time for bed," Hank said, "at least for me."

Walter was about to rise and go inside as well, but Laurel let her hand settle on his forearm.

"Thank you for playing your flute."

She searched for something more to say, but the words had been held inside too long. They would be heard by a man she didn't know, a man who even if he understood what she was trying to say, could not tell her so.

"I guess we'd best go on in," Laurel said. "I know you're tired."

It was Walter who rose first, but not before he'd settled his hand over hers a few moments, as though he had some inkling, Laurel thought, of what had been left unspoken.

CHAPTER NINE

"Where we going now, sir?" Wilber, the younger brother, asked.

Chauncey pointed to a building with wide steps and marble pillars.

"Is there another professor there we need to question, sir?" Jack asked.

"No, we just need to find which German books the library has."

"Do we have to write down all their names too?" Wilber whined.

"If you boys want to be dismissed, just say so and I'll take you home," Chauncey answered. "It's not something Paul Clayton would do but maybe you boys haven't got the soldier spirit like Paul."

"We got it, sir," Jack said, glaring at Wilber.

"All right then," Chauncey said, "but we need to go by the automobile first."

"That professor was shaking like a wet hound," Jack said as they walked across the campus. "He ought to be too, especially after he admitted his ownself he talked to them Germans with no one else around who understood them."

"I bet they got him to sneak secret messages back to Kaiser Wilhelm," Wilber said. "He could of hid them in that metal thing on his head."

"He'll not do it no more though," Jack said. "We sure set that professor straight. He won't be going back for no more visits. I bet he won't stir farther than he can throw his own shadow."

Chauncey couldn't help but let a smile lift the corners of his mouth. Professor Mayer had been scared. There was no doubt about that. Sweat had popped out on the old fool's brow even before claiming he'd gone to Hot Springs in the first place only because he'd been asked to read some of the Germans' letters. But Chauncey had outslicked him there, asking why he'd kept going back to socialize with a bunch of Huns. The professor's eyes had teared up and he'd started blubbering that it was a chance to practice his German. All the while the professor had the hearing machine clamped to his head, wires running this way and that and him fidgeting with the dial, which made him look even more ridiculous.

When they got to the Model T, Chauncey handed Jack the ledger and fountain pen and took off his belt and holster.

"Why are you doing that, sir?" Wilber asked.

"Because there's mostly women in libraries and real soldiers respect women. Seeing a pistol might give them the vapors."

As they walked toward the entrance, he thought of how his mother had wanted him to go to college. Chauncey, like his daddy, had argued he'd learn more about banking by being in one instead of a dusty classroom. Besides, he had never cottoned to school much, especially recess when other boys called him chicken when he wouldn't roughhouse. He hadn't been chicken. It was just that, unlike them, Chauncey had nice store-bought clothes he didn't want ruined.

When they came to the building that housed the library, Chauncey paused to study the letters chiseled above the thick oak doors. Latin or Greek, he knew, and thought how even during a war English wasn't good enough for the college. Chauncey nodded at the boys and the three of them went through the foyer and into the library wing. On the wall was a painting of an old man who didn't look that much different from Professor Mayer, though he didn't have the hearing gimcrack on his head. In front of the bookshelves were wooden desks and chairs. Some were occupied by students, their books and tablets splayed out before them as they slowly turned pages or dipped their pens into ink wells and wrote. The main desk was to the right. They moved to the room's center, the boys wide eyed at the tall ceilings and row after row of filled shelves. A male student came to the front desk with a book, an audible click as the librarian stamped the inside cover. It wasn't Miss Yount but a student assistant. A pretty young woman, another reason to be glad Miss Yount wasn't there. As the male student passed them on his way out, he didn't meet Chauncey's eyes. Too embarrassed, Chauncey knew, because he was hiding out at a college when real men were fighting a war. Chauncey looked beyond the tables and chairs to where books were lined up row after row as if poised for an attack.

"Come on," he told the boys.

As they passed the front desk, Chauncey saw that the student librarian was even prettier than he'd first thought, rosy cheeks and eyes a deep blue. Her perfume smelled like roses. She smiled at him and he was tempted to smile back but a serious demeanor was more appropriate. Still, Chauncey had obviously made a good impression. He'd come back some other time, without the boys. They went into the stacks and began checking book spines. He went through five shelves before he found letters that weren't English, but the books were in languages other than German. They've hidden them, he thought, but there were more foreign books on the next shelf. He found one that looked promising and compared it with the book confiscated from Professor Mayer. Chauncey studied the page in the library book first.

> *Das war ein Vorspiel nur, dort wo man Bücher*
> *verbrennt, verbrennt man auch am Ende Menschen.*

Then he looked at the professor's book.

> *Widerspreche ich mich?*
> *Na gut . . . ich widerspreche mich*
> *Ich bin geraümig . . . ich enthalte Massen.*

It was like deciphering a secret code as he searched for similar words. He looked farther down the pages and found one match and then another and then a third. He handed the library book to Jack and then others until both boys had their arms full.

"Take them over to an empty table," Chauncey said.

There were thirty-seven. Chauncey opened his ledger and took out the fountain pen he'd used at the savings and loan.

Customers noticed the pen's gold cap and gold bands but, more important, they saw how solid and sturdy the pen was, and by extension the institution itself. When Chauncey wrote up a payment or a loan, he didn't have to keep dipping the pen in an inkwell like a chicken pecking corn. His words flowed with a steady assurance. He wrote *Mars Hill Library* on the ledger's second page, skipped a line, and began copying book titles. The language looked sinister, especially the two dots that resembled a rattlesnake bite. The words could mean anything.

He peeked over at the front desk. The pretty student was still there but now Miss Yount had joined her. It seemed the old hag had been around Mars Hill forever and everyone kowtowed to her. She had a sharp tongue and no qualms about using it on anyone from a sassy child to Preacher Wilkenson. Miss Yount was tall too, especially with her hair balled up on her head. Jack handed him the last book and he wrote down the title. The table was covered with books and Chauncey thought how he'd be doing a service for Mars Hill and the whole country if he took a match and dropped it on them. Old and dusty as they were, they'd burn quick as that Hun zeppelin did in New Jersey. As he closed the ledger, Chauncey glimpsed his letter to Governor Bickett. He reminded himself to mail it before he took Traveler out for an afternoon gallop.

"We've done important work today," Chauncey said and capped the fountain pen. "Maybe it's not so exciting but lots of times that's the way it is in the army. Even at the front you spend more of your time waiting than shooting or bayoneting the enemy."

They were walking toward the door when Miss Yount came around her desk and blocked their departure.

"What are you doing?"

Chauncey didn't like Miss Yount being so close. She smelled of horehound and talc and her hair hovered over him like a cannonball. The steel-rimmed glasses made her eyes big and bulgy.

"I was checking for books that might be written to aid the enemy."

"Did you find any?" Miss Yount asked. "If so, I'll need to take them out of fiction and poetry and shelve them in the rhetoric section."

Chauncey glanced over at the front desk and saw the young librarian listened.

"I won't know until I send the titles to Washington," Chauncey answered, putting some barb in his voice too.

"Be that as it may," Miss Yount said, "you aren't leaving this library until those books are shelved and in the right order."

Chauncey met her eyes, knowing she expected him to cower like some snotty-nosed brat or lackey at the general store. He kept his eyes right on hers and didn't blink.

"I am not a student, Miss Yount. I am a soldier."

"A soldier," she said. "Then why aren't you in Europe?"

Chauncey knew his face reddened but he wasn't going to look down or to the side or anywhere else besides into her ugly old gogglified eyes.

"These boys need to go home," he said. "They have their evening chores to do."

"You won't need them," Miss Yount answered.

Chauncey thought about stepping around her but he knew she'd block him and that would only make it worse. He noticed the student librarian still smiled, but it wasn't a nice smile like earlier.

"Go outside and wait for me," he told the boys. "I need to talk to Miss Yount alone."

"Yeah," Jack said, his voice sullen.

Chauncey waited for the boys to get through the door.

"I'd not normally do this, but I will this time."

He didn't look at the student librarian as he passed the main desk. Chauncey thought about whistling to show putting the books back didn't bother him one whit. But as he placed the books on the shelf, a better idea came to him. He turned so Miss Yount couldn't see and took out his fountain pen. On the first page of a book, he wrote *Miss Yount is a Hun loving* . . . Chauncey paused. It was a word he had heard only a couple of times and never seen spelled. Either way, she'll know what it means, he figured, and wrote *kunt*. He set the book back and wedged Professor Mayer's book onto the shelf as well.

Chauncey paused as he passed the front desk.

"A student wrote something real nasty about you in one of the German books, Miss Yount," he said, loud enough that everyone from the pretty student to the old fogey in the painting heard it.

The boys waited on the steps. They stood when Chauncey came out but there was a slouching insolence to their posture.

"Are we going to get to go home now?" Jack asked.

"Are we going to get to go home now, *sir*," Chauncey said sharply.

CHAPTER TEN

A misty drizzle fell all morning. Fog tendriled out of the woods, slow wisps merging and unfurling across the cove floor. As the day wore on, the fog thickened. The hammer's steady taps sounded farther and farther away. When Laurel walked to the springhouse to get milk, Hank and Walter were immersed in the whiteness. All she could see was the scarecrow, its arms raised above the swirling fog as if in rising water. She had clothed it in the tattered shirt and pants Walter had worn into the cove. The hammering stopped, probably to measure the strands for the next section, but as Laurel stared at the scarecrow she had the sensation that time had somehow unwoven and it was again last fall. Hank was still in Europe and Walter was nothing more than a figment her loneliness had fleshed out from a cross of wood and tattered cloth. Laurel thought of the silver flute, how she had held it in her hand, solid beyond any dream. The hammering began again but once back at the cabin she opened the case and pressed two fingers firm against the silver. But it won't be here tomorrow, she thought.

Laurel fetched a jar of blackberries from the larder and cinnamon and sugar from her tins rack, made a pie, and placed it in the oven. The washtub was on the porch so she carried it to her room, poured in water from the kettle and the well. She undressed and scrunched herself into the tub. Like always, bathing was a soothing thing, so she lingered a minute, felt the water drip off her hair and down her back, took in the clean clear smell of the soap on her skin. After Laurel toweled herself dry, she got the blue-and-white gingham dress from the closet, its broad shoulders widened to help conceal the purple stain. She'd sewn the dress last fall for the night she and Jubel were to meet at the Ledfords' barn. She tied the blue ribbon in her hair and sweetened her skin and breath with lilac and licorice root, rubbed cardinal flower petals on her neck though it seemed not to have had much of an effect.

Laurel turned to the mirror and it was like seeing herself for the first time in ever so long, because she was looking at her whole self, not just her face or hair but each part of her, slowly making her way down to her waist. With the birth stain covered, she could almost believe someone might find her pretty. She looked in the mirror a few more moments and then took the tub to the porch and emptied it, came back inside and finished making supper.

After a while she heard Hank and Walter on the porch and brought them towels. They took off their boots and unhitched their overalls to the waist, sharing a bucket of water thickened with Borax, then used Hank's pocket comb to roach back their soggy hair. They stood by the hearth barefoot, patting water off their faces.

"Damn if don't feel like I've been bobbing in water all day," Hank said. "A drizzle like that damps a man deeper than a hard rain for sure, but we got that upper section finished."

Hank threw a handful of kindling in the hearth and the fire leaped up as if startled.

"It's a drearisome day like this that makes a fellow appreciate coming in to a warm fire and warm food," Hank said. "And look at sister there, all spangled out in a pretty dress. There's worser ends to a man's day, don't you reckon, Walter?"

Laurel's face flushed, though she reckoned she should be used to it. Hank had been saying things like that the last two days, giving all sorts of compliments to her in front of Walter, everything from Laurel's sewing to how bonny her hair was. Then last night, Hank had gone to bed early, leaving her and Walter alone on the porch. Needing Walter's help so bad he'd even try to play Cupid to get him to stay on. Yet maybe it was more than just that, Laurel thought. Maybe Hank wanted for her what he had with Carolyn, and figured a man like Walter might be the best chance of her ever having it.

She set the bread basket on the table and she and the men sat down. As they ate, Laurel heard the ticking of Hank's pocket watch, something she'd hardly made notice of before. But she heard it now, couldn't make herself not hear it as Hank talked about all the farm improvements left to do. Every second was one less Walter would be here.

"I wish you weren't going," Hank said as Laurel served dessert. "It's nice having steady help. If you could stay on a couple more months, we could get that pasture fenced and the well dug. I'll even raise your pay to a dollar fifty a day. Plus I bet Laurel would keep making these pies. She never makes them when it's just me around."

Laurel blushed.

"I've made plenty of pies for you."

"None this good though," Hank said, holding up a piece on a fork.

"So you think we could change your mind?" Hank asked.

Walter smiled slightly but shook his head.

"I was afraid of that," Hank said. "I guess life in New York is a little more lively than being in the back of beyond."

"Would you play your flute for us tonight?" Laurel asked as they rose from the table. "We'll not likely hear such pretty music in this cove again."

"That would be nice," Hank agreed.

They went out on the porch and she sat beside Walter. He raised the flute to his lips. At first Laurel thought he was just practicing, because the same few notes he started with kept repeating with just the smallest changes. Then it became clear that it was a song, the loneliest sort of song because the notes changed so little, like one bird calling and waiting for another to answer. It was as lonely a sound as she'd ever heard. Walter took the flute from his lips, held it before him as if to show that, once freed from his breath, the flute was silent as he was. Laurel lifted a kerchief from her dress pocket and dabbed her eyes. Hank too seemed stirred by the song. A sadness came over his face and he lowered his eyes. Walter shut the flute inside the case.

"If everyone could make sounds that beautiful, we'd never want to speak," Laurel said. "We could just call to each other, let each other know we weren't alone."

"That's a pretty thought, sister," Hank said, "but I expect there'd still be plenty who'd rather use that silver to bash each other's heads in."

Hank rose from the railing and stretched his arms.

"It seems you've decided, but if you change your mind, we'd love to have you stay on, even if it's just another week."

"You could stay longer," Laurel said after Hank went inside, "but I guess you need to get back to New York. Are there people waiting for you, besides the people you play music with? I mean like some kinfolks, or a sweetheart?"

Walter shook his head.

"I was always of a mind to leave here," Laurel said. "My teacher Miss Calicut claimed I had enough smarts to go off somewhere like Asheville or Raleigh and be a teacher or secretary or most anything I'd want. But Daddy was sick and I didn't have a choice but to stay. It's like I've never had a single choice in my life. Most people get at least a few choices, don't they?"

Walter nodded. Even though Hank had gone inside, it was like she could still hear the watch mark each passing moment.

"It'd be nice if you could talk but it's ever so good just to have someone listen. What you say with your head nods is enough." Laurel's voice softened. "I'd not ever want more."

Brashy words, she told herself, but at least you'll have your say. You'll not look back when he's gone and wonder if there was the least chance you could have swayed him. If he gets up and goes inside right now, doesn't listen to one word more, it'll still be better than not having said it.

"They's folks who won't set foot in this cove. They think nothing good can happen here. I'd come to believe them. But you came here, and that's been good. There's been some good in it for you too, hasn't there?"

When Walter nodded, Laurel left her chair. She stood in front of him and reached for his hands.

"Will you hold me for a minute? That way it'll help me remember you were real, because once you leave it'll be too easy to believe you weren't."

Laurel trembled as she placed her head against his chest, her arms tight around his waist. She stayed that way, feeling the sound of his heartbeat. He raised a hand and settled it on her shoulder. She lifted her lips, not sure if he'd let her kiss him. But he did, his lips meeting hers. Then he freed his hand from her shoulder and stepped back. Laurel led the way to his door with the lantern. Let it be enough, Laurel told herself. There's been times you'd not believe you could have even this much.

CHAPTER ELEVEN

As black shallowed to gray in the cabin window, he thought of what Goritz had said about needing to suffer. Easier not to see Laurel, he had decided, so quietly dressed and made his way to the door by tentative steps and touches, the haversack on his shoulder. Outside, there was little light until the trail curled around the cliff face and the sky unsealed into a wide leveling dawn. At the trail notch, he passed under dangles of glass tied to a tree limb. He thought again of the hanged man.

Slidell met him on the porch.

"Didn't expect you this early. I got to eat and then we can go. Come inside and I'll fix you something too."

Walter shook his head.

"All right, I'll be out in a few minutes."

As he waited on the steps, he thought how amazing it was that three years in New York had passed before he and the others were rounded up. They had been able to leave the harbor day or night and go wherever they pleased. They swam in the Hudson River in the summer and skated in Central Park in the fall. Because the crew still got paid, they could attend concerts and operas, enjoy good food and good drink. Some of his fellow musicians spent evenings on River Street, playing patriotic songs between rousing speeches. There was plenty of time to do such things because, for the musicians at least, they performed only an occasional fund-raiser. For those three years, the ship and its crew had been as safe there as any place in the world. IN HEAVEN, an onboard banner had proclaimed one October night.

It would be different now, but Goritz was surely still there, and willing to help him.

Slidell came out and they got in the wagon and left. The wagon bumped and jostled out of the yard and onto a path little wider than the wheels. The woods thickened and the blue sky disappeared. Walter checked his pocket and confirmed that he still had the note for the depot manager, only then realized he'd left the medallion. Better not to have it on him anyway. They were coming out of deep woods when Slidell spoke.

"Them you stayed with are good folks, and the way they been maligned, especially that girl, is a grievous sin, and once Hank's married it's going to make it all the harder. I wish she could find someone the way Hank has. Men ought to be lined up with all she's got to offer, including her prettiness, though folks make her think it's not so because of that birth stain. Don't you think she's pretty?"

Walter nodded because he was expected to, but also because it was true.

Slidell jostled the checkreins and looked straight ahead.

"Forgive an old man for speaking his mind, but I could tell the other night she'd taken a shine to you, seemed you'd taken a bit of a shine to her too. I was hoping you all might get to sparking and it change your mind about leaving."

Leaving. He would be the one this time, remembering the English ocean liner that had harbored only meters from his own ship. There had been quite a bustle when the liner departed. All morning cars and carriages brought passengers and steamer trunks shipside. When the rain let up, he'd left his own ship and sat on the pier as the dockworkers untied the ropes tethering ship to shore. Tugboats arrived to nudge the liner into the Hudson as the last passengers boarded and the pier's crowd waved handkerchiefs and hurled confetti. He had brought the flute but did not play until a young woman in a green silk dress, matching parasol in hand, paused on the gangplank and looked his way. She nodded at the flute, mouthed the word *Brahms*. He raised the silver to his lips and began the final movement of the First Symphony. The flute's notes soared over the ruckus around them. The woman placed her free hand on the railing and let the parasol settle on her shoulder. She was young, probably no more than twenty, tall and slim, her long black hair accentuating her ivory-white skin. She nodded slightly, knowingly, as the song crested and then faded. The last of the voyagers came up the gangplank, passed first the woman and then a steward who checked off names. The steward came to escort her onto the deck but the woman remained where she was, as if the music might yet woo her back to shore.

The song ended and she smiled and spoke but again her

words were lost in the confusion of other voices. He raised a hand to his ear and made his way toward the gangplank, not taking his eyes off her as she pointed him out to the steward and said something. She walked on up the gangplank as the steward walked down. Walter pushed through the riotous crowd until he and the steward were face-to-face. *The young lady said that she hopes you will play for her again, perhaps when the ship makes its return voyage next month.* The steward made his way back aboard as the ocean liner's steam horn announced the voyage had begun. Walter had turned back into the mob then, searching for her among the passengers offering their farewells. As the water widened between them, he saw the parasol's green rounding amid the jostling of Mephisto feathers and top hats. He watched until the parasol was just a dot of green and then not even that. The next day he went to the Cunard Line's office and checked the ship's return date. It was a week later when he had seen the headline LUSITANIA SUNK BY HUNS.

They came to a better-maintained road and Slidell tugged the left rein and the horse turned that way. The blue sky reappeared, wider and brighter than Walter had seen in two weeks. After so long its vastness was disconcerting. They passed cabins and houses and before much longer he saw a clock tower and brick and wood buildings huddled on a hilltop.

"That's the college. It's named Mars Hill too. It ain't very big so I doubt you ever heard of it."

Walter had heard of it but did not nod as the road leveled and then began its descent into the village. Slidell hitched the horse to a post in front of a café and pointed up the street.

"There's the depot. I'm going over to the hardware store and after that I'll be yonder in the Turkey Trot," Slidell said, pointing to a low-slung building beyond the depot. "If you change your mind, I'll be in town at least till noon."

Walter nodded and stepped onto the boardwalk. He passed the café and a clothing store and then a barbershop, the white-smocked barber outside on a bench, his face obscured by a newspaper.

The barber lowered his paper.

"You need a haircut?"

Walter shook his head and went on. The boardwalk ended and train tracks lined the road edge, on them a freight train whose coal car was being filled. On the depot's platform, two old men on a bench stared at a checkerboard. The redcap leaned against a post, cleaning the underside of his nails with a pocketknife. Walter stepped inside to buy his ticket. A woman with a child no more than four or five stood at the window, the depot master explaining a train's arrival time. The child saw him and let go of his mother's hand, walked over to a wanted poster tacked on the far wall. For a few moments Walter simply stared at the sketch of his own face. No scraggly beard appeared on the drawing, but his face was clearly recognizable. He felt not a constriction in his chest but a hollowness, as if his heart had simply evaporated. The child ran to his mother and tugged her hand. The woman spoke brusquely to the child, then turned back to the depot master.

Head down, Walter went out the door. He stepped off the platform and to the building's side where he was alone. He had no trouble feeling his heart now. It pumped frantically as he tried to contain his fear enough to decide what to do. The coal bin was almost full so the train would leave soon. To where he had no idea but surely far enough away that his face wouldn't be on the depot wall. He walked head down past the linked boxcars until he found one with an open side door. He was about to dive in when a Pinkerton stepped from behind the caboose, billy club in hand. The guard smiled and tapped the wood against his palm.

The Pinkerton did not follow so at least he hadn't been recognized. Walter walked rapidly up the boardwalk, fighting the impulse to break into a run. He raised his eyes only to make furtive glances for suspicious stares, more wanted posters, saw none. He passed the last storefront and settled himself behind the college's marble arch. The railroad tracks glistened in the late-morning light. Thirty meters at most, but it was all open ground. The Pinkerton could be anywhere, at the depot or walking behind the caboose or on the train itself. He looked around for a metal rod or hefty stick, saw nothing.

The train gave two quick whistle blasts and the cut steel wheels made their first halting turns. Stay where you are and you'll soon be hanging from this arch, he told himself, and patted the haversack to ensure that the flute case was there. A stack of railroad ties lay halfway between the marble arch and the tracks. If he got there unseen, the sprint to an open boxcar would be only two or three seconds. Walter hunched over and ran, flung himself down behind the ties. His gasped breaths sounded so loud he closed his mouth and breathed through his nose, taking in the acrid smell of creosote. He glanced toward the depot but didn't see the Pinkerton. He peeked over the ties and saw the cowcatcher and then the engineer with an elbow propped on the windowsill. When the coal car passed, he glanced toward the depot a last time and rose, looked down the tracks for the first open boxcar.

He saw the Pinkerton before the Pinkerton saw him. The guard stood inside the open car, one hand on the metal door and the other wielding the billy club. As Walter began running, he heard a menacing shout but dared not look back. He passed the college entrance and ran up the road away from town, cresting the hill before slowing to a fast walk. An automobile soon came up behind him. Too winded to run anymore, he kept his head down, waited to hear if it stopped and men poured out to strike the first blow. But the automobile did not pause. The road curved and woods appeared on the right side. He entered them twice to hide before the turnoff appeared and he followed it. After a while he came to Slidell's house and then followed the trail down the cliff side and back into the cove.

III

CHAPTER TWELVE

As they approached Doak Ellenburg's barn, milking traces jostled the wagon's iron-rimmed wheels, swayed the buckboard Hank and Laurel shared with Slidell. Doak Ellenburg and his wife Hester had farmed this land before opening their livery stable in Mars Hill. Wesley, their only child, had been the first soldier killed from Madison County. No body had been shipped home from France, no last unmailed letter or watch or wallet.

"Looks to be a good portion of folks here tonight," Slidell said after he pulled the brake and tied the checkreins.

"I wish we'd talked Walter into coming," Hank said. "You

could of brought your guitar and these folks would hear something special."

"He's shy around people because he can't talk," Laurel said.

"He's been here two months," Hank said. "It ain't going to get any easier if he don't try."

"Give him time," Slidell said. "Shy ain't near the worst thing a man can be, whether he can or can't talk."

Slidell and Hank lifted the bulging tow sacks and walked past other wagons and buggies, two Model Ts. Near the entrance, what looked like an enormous poppet doll sprawled in the weedy dirt. The shirt and pants were thatched with straw, a rotting pumpkin set atop the shirt collar. Drawn on the pumpkin were daggered teeth beneath a mustache and a monocle. A pitchfork jabbed through the chest, as if the effigy might try to slither away. KAISER BILL, a placard proclaimed.

Inside, red, white, and blue streamers dangled from the rafters, the sideboards arrayed with Liberty Bond posters of American soldiers leaving home, hulking Germans with spiked helmets, Lady Liberty with flag in hand. But the poster that held Laurel's eye was the one with a huge blood-red handprint, below it the words

THE HUN—HIS MARK
BLOT IT OUT
WITH
LIBERTY BONDS

Hank's hand, Laurel thought, bloody and bodiless, still somewhere in France. She wondered if it was the poster Hank noticed first, and saw his own hand hovering ghostlike before him.

Laurel gathered their coats and draped them on a stall door.

When she came back, Doak sorted what Hank and Slidell had given him into boxes marked SCRAP IRON and RUBBER. Grief can age a body quicker than time, Laurel's mother had once told her, and she saw the truth of it and not only in Doak Ellenburg's face. His shoulders curved inward, his back was hunched. Slidell had said the arrival of the dust-colored Western Union telegram had so grieved Doak's wife that she hardly ever left the house, even for the jubilees.

"You young folks go mingle," Slidell said. "I saw Ansel's and Boyce's horses so I'm figuring there to be some sipping going on behind this barn."

"I might have a sampling myself later," Hank replied. "If we get too walleyed, Laurel can stack us in the back and drive us home."

"Looks like the Weatherbees aren't here yet," Laurel said after Slidell left.

"You ever known it to be different?" Hank grumbled. "That old man's contrary to any kind of fandango, even when it's for a good cause. Soon as he gets here he's ready to turn around. But there ain't no changing him. I've learned that."

Laurel looked for Marcie Bettingfield but saw instead Jubel Parton talking to his friends. Jubel saw Laurel as well and quickly dropped his gaze. He spoke to one of his friends a moment and then walked out of the barn. Laurel knew he wouldn't be back. Afraid Hank would thrash him again and maybe afraid of her too. The night Jubel had won his bet, she'd washed the blood from her thighs and gone in the barn to tell Slidell she was sick and needed to go home. As Laurel had searched for Slidell, she'd seen Jubel looking her way. She'd waved a hand across her face, then pointed an index finger at Jubel and made a circling motion. Nothing but a made-up pretend curse, but Jubel's face had paled. Laurel had taken some pleasure in that, if for no other reason than wiping the smirk off his face. He'd better be glad I'm not a witch, she'd thought that night, because I'd put a suffering on him like he's never known. But Hank had made Jubel pay.

"I still say Walter should of come," Hank said. "He won't get over his skittishness unless he's around folks."

"I want to teach him how to read and write," Laurel said. "That might confidence him more."

Ezra Davenport came up to Hank, his gnarly face grim as he nodded toward the barn's rear.

"You seen what them Hun bastards done to my grandboy?"

"I didn't know he was back," Hank said.

"Got home yesterday," Ezra said. "Them sons of bitches gassed him."

Laurel followed Hank to where several men were gathered around Michael Davenport, who'd been conscripted the same week as Hank. Black patches covered his eyes, the silky cloth held in place by a string knotted behind his head. Burn scars welted his face and neck and phlegm clotted each breath. A white cane leaned against a barn slat.

Hank took Michael's hand in his and leaned close, spoke so softly no one except Michael heard. But only the words were soft. Hank had never said if he'd killed men in France, but Laurel saw enough hatred in his face now to believe he could have. Michael's brothers flanked their younger sibling, their faces as grim as their grandfather's. As Hank exchanged handshakes with the brothers, Michael's head turned slowly left to right, as if looking over the crowd. Maybe reacting to the sounds, Laurel thought, but it was as if his body hadn't yet realized his sight had been doused forever. Michael started coughing and the brothers clutched him by the arms as Ezra retrieved the white cane.

"We got to get him home," Ezra said. "That gas has festered his lungs and he can't near swallow nor breathe."

Clusters parted so the brothers could pass three astride. Michael shuffled his feet, head still turning left and right as his siblings guided him toward the barn mouth.

"What did you say to Michael?" Laurel asked.

"That if they'd let me back in the army I'd kill a dozen of those Huns for what they done to him. Boyce is right. There's things people ought not do to each other, even in a war. When I was over there I heard awful stories, babies stabbed with bayonets, a Hun general who'd filled a tub with eyeballs. I never saw such and figured it just tall tales. Even what happened to me, I figured it was just one sorry son of a bitch. But now . . ."

Hank shook his head.

"I'm going to have a big swallow of that white liquor before the Weatherbees get here. Maybe that'll help smooth my dander."

Hank went outside as Ansel and Boyce Clayton came up on the makeshift stage. A guitarist and Lee Ellen, Boyce's wife, were with them, Lee Ellen's voice blending with her husband's.

> The news has flashed around
> Our boys are homeward bound
> Skies of gray have given way to brightness
> Hearts that once were sad are feeling gay
> And we'll be there to meet them just to say
> Oh welcome welcome you are welcome home.

As the song ended, a child running ahead of her mother bumped into Laurel. She was about to help her up when the mother snatched the child's arm so Laurel couldn't touch her.

The mother glared and dragged her daughter away. The Claytons finished two more songs before Marcie entered the barn, her baby cradled in one arm. She waved and hugged the baby closer as she and Laurel made their way to each other. Even at a distance, Laurel saw how having a baby had changed Marcie, her bosom and hips bigger but a gauntness in her face. Laurel remembered how pretty she'd been in the cotton batiste wedding dress. Her sisters had adorned Marcie's brown hair with virgin's bower and when she'd walked down the church aisle her tresses were bright and pretty as winter stars. Laurel had been there to see it, because Marcie had told Robbie there'd be no wedding unless Laurel was invited. It had taken a lot of sand to do that but Marcie had always had plenty of sand.

They met in front of the stage and leaned into a half hug.

"Where's Robbie?"

"Outside talking with some of his buddies, probably sipping moonshine too. I'll oblige him that though. He's been hanging tobacco since the pink of day."

The baby whined and Marcie patted him, set his head on her shoulder.

"I just give you a good feeding, boy. This one ain't to be satisfied, Laurel. Some days I'm of a mind to wear a cowbell for all the suckling he does, and Robbie already wanting another, but he ain't the one got a chap tugging on his teat all day."

"You're still tonicing with that Queen Anne's lace?" Laurel asked.

"I am and it's working," Marcie said, and smiled, "because we've given it a bushel full of testings."

The song ended and Chauncey Feith came onto the stage as the Claytons stepped off. He wore his wool uniform though the barn was warm. A gun was holstered around his waist, as if

Germans might rush through the barn mouth at any moment. Laurel watched as six boys settled behind Chauncey, arms by their sides. They were fresh scrubbed, their hair clean and combed, and Chauncey had dressed them up in khaki pants and blue denim shirts, thin black belts and black socks. But the well-worn brogans, several pairs passed down from larger feet, showed they were farm kids. They tried to act grown up but grins kept widening their pressed lips. Laurel saw Hank by the barn mouth, his eyes on the stage too.

Chauncey Feith raised his arms and the barn grew quiet. One of the boys handed him some sheets of paper and Chauncey began to read.

"It is gratifying to see all of you here, and I commend your unceasing support of war bonds and the scrap metal and rubber drive. As the song says, I also hope that our brave men are indeed homeward bound. There are continued good tidings from Europe and some say this war could end soon, but we have heard that before. Whatever news of victory we hear or read, we cannot rest until the kaiser hangs from a rope in that fancy palace of his. We must remain ever vigilant, because the Hun will become even more desperate and devious, not just overseas but here in Madison County, where we of late have all but been overrun with likely imperial agents. Thus I offer the following."

Chauncey raised his eyes and shuffled the papers.

"To President Lange and the board of trustees. We the following demand the immediate removal of Doctor Horatio Mayer from his position as Professor of Languages at Mars Hill College. Furthermore, we demand that he not be allowed on the campus in any capacity, especially to have contact with students. We know for a fact that Professor Mayer has conversed with men we have cause to believe are enemy spies, a matter that has already been reported to you. Information passed to him could cost American lives. Professor Mayer must be immediately dismissed from the college. Let us not hear any more cries about free speech, that colleges should embrace any and all sorts of free thinking. Professor Mayer does not have the right to speak freely when his allegiances are not our own or, we surely hope, the college he represents. His continued employment will cause everlasting dishonor to Mars Hill College. Furthermore, Miss Dorothea Yount should be, at the very least, severely reprimanded for her allowance of potentially subversive books in the campus library. We would note that a number of your own faculty have already agreed to sign this petition. Their having done so is an act of true courage. Let Professor Mayer's dismissal be the first step in restoring Mars Hill College's honor and good name."

Chauncey raised his eyes.

"The boys have already placed copies of this petition on Doak's table. If you believe in freedom, sign the petition. Thank you for coming tonight and for all your contributions for our brave soldiers."

Chauncey gave a crisp salute, the boys following him single file as the Claytons stepped back on the stage and began "The False Knight," a song Laurel had always liked. If Walter had come, he could play it for her later, though the main reason she'd wish him here was simply missing him. How could she not when for two months they'd been in the cove together every day, every night on the porch alone for at least a few minutes, holding hands and exchanging brief kisses.

"The Weatherbees are here," Marcie said, nodding toward the barn mouth where Carolyn's parents talked to an older couple.

Hank stood beside Carolyn, who was all spruced up in a blue cotton dress and white Buster Brown collar. Her face had been roughened by acne but there was a prettiness in her blue eyes and copper-colored hair. Smart as a whip too, Hank claimed. Easy enough to see why he was smitten by her. The Claytons played a slower song and Hank took Carolyn's hand, placed his forearm and stubbed wrist against her back and pulled her close. She settled her head against Hank's chest and they joined the other couples on the makeshift dance floor. Laurel was about to tell Marcie about Walter but Marcie spoke first.

"Not marrying Carolyn until he fixes up the farm for you is an honorable thing," Marcie said. "Good of Carolyn too, especially since her daddy's giving them that land on Balsam. There's many a woman who'd want her betrothed working on her house, not his sister's."

I don't know your meaning, Laurel almost said, but then she did know, and the wonder was that she hadn't realized before. The Claytons continued to play but like the talk of adults and the cries of babies and shouts of children the music seemed distant, as though the world was pulling away from her. Marcie sighed as the baby nuzzled her breast.

"I best go suckle him, because it'll be a sight easier now than on a bumpy wagon. Maybe he'll sleep a bit too. That way I can swaddle him in a corner and give me and Robbie a chance to dance a song or two. It's been ever so long since we've done that."

Laurel nodded and Marcie left. When had Hank planned to tell her? When the furniture arrived at the train station and was hauled north to Balsam instead of into the cove? Fixing up the farm for her, Marcie had said, but Hank had also done it to prove to Carolyn and her daddy that, even with one hand, Hank could do the work needed to support a wife and family. He had used part of his army savings but also the last of the money their parents left behind. She thought of the new fence with its taut strands and metal thorns and how Slidell had mentioned the expense of barbed wire instead of split rails. Hank had said barbed wire lasted so much longer. With a small gasp, Laurel realized something else—that Hank was making it clear he'd not ask Laurel to live with him and Carolyn. She would be left behind, and he had decided that months ago.

A mute man might take a wife no one else wanted, a man who didn't know what others believed about Laurel. I'm helping you as much as I can, sister, Hank would figure each night he left her and Walter alone on the porch or bragged on Laurel's cooking or sewing, hoping to get shed of what he was too ashamed to tell her. There had been girls before the war who'd not spark with Hank because, though no purple stain marked him, they believed the cove's bad luck did. Then he'd lost the hand and there were women who'd not want him because of that. But he'd found one who would share a life with him, as long as that life was outside the cove. He'd had a choice, maybe the only one Hank figured to ever get, and he'd chosen. Choose Walter, or choose being alone. She'd drunk the tonic with Queen Anne's lace for a month now, and marked her bleeds on the calendar from Mr. Shuler's store. There was a choice in the doing of that too, and a hoping. But would Walter choose her?

The Weatherbees had left. Hank and Slidell can drink on the wagon easy as behind a barn, Laurel told herself, so she got all the coats and went outside, found the men with their backs against the graying side boards, legs spraddled before them. An empty quart mason jar lay close by.

"I think I just saw a second moon, Laurel," Slidell said.

"I think I see more than one myself," Hank agreed.

"We need to go," Laurel said.

Hank fished the watch from his pocket, angled it to catch what light slanted between the barn planks.

"It ain't even ten yet, sister."

Laurel nodded at the mason jar.

"You've drained that so there's no cause to stay longer."

Slidell lifted the mason jar, apprised it indeed empty.

"I guess it is time," Slidell said.

Hank helped him to his feet. The older man leaned his shoulder against the barn, one hand flat against the boards.

"This barn shifts like a weathervane," he said.

"You keep him upright," Laurel told Hank. "I'll bring the wagon."

It wasn't the first time she'd driven home from a jubilee, so Ginny was comfortable when Laurel took the checkreins in hand and brought the wagon to where the men waited. Laurel spread wool horse blankets across the bed boards and she and Hank lifted Slidell into the wagon. Hank pushed until Slidell's knees bent enough to hitch the gate.

"You sober enough to stay on the buckboard, or do you need to crawl in there with him?" Laurel asked.

"I can stay on," Hank said.

Laurel lit the lantern and pulled up her coat collar. Not the coldest night they'd had this fall but cold enough. She jerked the reins and the wagon rolled away from the music and voices. Soon the only sounds were the creak of jostled wood and Slidell's moans when the wagon bumped over a milking trace. A waxing moon dusted everything beneath in a silvery light. Always so pretty, Laurel thought, not just the moon but the wide pasture of stars that made the sky so much larger than in the cove.

Laurel didn't speak until they were on the pike.

"Marcie told me you and Carolyn are setting up house on Balsam."

"Carolyn's daddy won't abide her living in the cove," Hank said after a few moments. "That's why he's giving us the twenty acres."

"It seems most everybody knew that but me."

"I was going to tell you," Hank said. "It just never seemed the right time."

There was more she could say, and say in an accusing tone, but she suddenly felt too tired to bother.

"If you were in my shoes, you'd not do the same?" Hank asked after a while.

"I've never had that chance, have I?"

"You've got it now," Hank answered.

"How do you know he'd even want me?"

"Because I ain't got two hands but I do have two eyes," Hank said. "You know well as I do that he came back because of you."

"I don't know that for sure. How can I if he can't say it?"

"Dammit, Laurel, why else would he? To bust his ass all week for what he can probably make one night tooting a fife? Because he likes being in a gloamy cove?"

When they got to Slidell's, Laurel unhitched Ginny and led her to the barn while Hank helped Slidell into the house. Hank returned with the lantern they'd left for the walk back. Hank hung the lantern on his forearm, struck a match, and lit the wick before handing it to her.

"I'm staying here tonight."

Laurel walked out of the yard, the lantern held before her. Soon the moon and stars vanished as the trail began its descent. She counted back the days to her last bleed because it wouldn't be like Jubel with his rubber sheath. It seemed a safe time, especially since she'd been drinking the tonic. There'd be some women who'd hope they weren't fallow. They'd think getting with child would snare Walter into staying, but Laurel knew of men who'd seeded a chap and then run off. They'd left behind their kin and work and sometimes even farms, lots more than what Walter would leave. You may be putting the cart before the horse, she told herself, thinking how the earlier times when Hank had left, she and Walter were so skittish around each other they hadn't even kissed. The trail dropped sharply and Laurel swept the lantern low over her feet to see each coming step. After a while the trail leveled and the woods thickened.

No light came from the porch, but as Laurel approached, the flute's music filtered through the trees as if to guide her. She let it, no longer looking at the trail. As Laurel walked into the yard, the song changed to the one Walter had played on the Friday night eight weeks ago. A farewell song then, but now it welcomed her. Even if he can never say a word, even if there's no one to speak to for weeks at a time, he can play for me. That'll be enough, Laurel vowed. I'll never want more, and if I do I'll make myself remember what it was like here alone. She wasn't sure who she was swearing it to—herself or God or Walter, maybe the cove itself. Only when her foot touched the porch step did the song cease. Walter sat in a chair, wearing a coat Hank had given him. He set the flute in its case and closed the lid. His face showed dimly in the lantern light.

"Hank is staying at Slidell's tonight."

Laurel placed the lantern on the railing and sat down. She thought about taking his hand but didn't. Don't wait, she told herself, if you do you'll not say it at all.

"I want to tell you something," Laurel said, and took a breath, let it out slowly. "I have feelings for you, heart feelings. I need to know if you feel that way about me."

At first it seemed Walter hadn't heard. Then he nodded, almost reluctantly it seemed, but his hand settled over hers. Laurel turned her hand and their palms met. His hand was cold as hers. She felt calluses that, like the thickened muscles in his arms and chest, hadn't been there in August.

"So you feel the same for me?"

Walter nodded.

Minutes passed and they both seemed afraid to make the slightest move, as if between their clasping hands was a moth or mayfly, something so fragile a touch could damage it. Walter leaned and kissed her softly on the mouth, let go of her hand. He stood and walked into the cabin.

Laurel lifted the lantern and went to the privy, then came inside. As she passed Walter's door, the lantern's glow revealed it half ajar, but that also meant half closed. Laurel went to her room and set the lamp on the bed table, took off her dress and shoes and put on her gown. She sat on the bed and stared at the inch-thick wall. So close, three feet of emptiness and a couple of wooden planks. She almost rose to place her hand on the wall. That way she could imagine Walter doing the same.

Instead, Laurel snuffed the lantern. Though she was cold and the quilts would warm her, she did not lie down but remained sitting on the bed. She began shivering, unsure if it was just the cold. A few minutes later she heard the rasp of corn shucks. Walter had lain down or gotten up. His door creaked and Laurel waited. The footsteps paused at her open door. Getting his bearings, unsure what might be in the room, for as far as she knew he'd never been in it. That or still deciding.

"I'm here," Laurel said softly, and pulled back the covers, lay down, and made room.

CHAPTER THIRTEEN

Hank left for the Weatherbees' house early Sunday morning. *I'll likely not be back till dark*, he'd told Laurel, making clear that, as on Friday night, she and Walter would be alone a long while. Walter had come to her room after Hank left. Afterward Laurel hadn't put her gown back on. Instead, she'd spooned herself into him, Walter's chest against her back, knees tucked close and his arm over her hip. The quilt was pulled only to their waists and Laurel let it remain so, his body a more soothing warmth.

Outside, it began to rain, at first a few slow drops tapping the tin roof, a sound much like yesterday when Hank and Walter boarded up the windows. Laurel had welcomed the hammer's steady taps, because it signaled Walter's presence. So different from the previous fall with her father newly dead and Hank still in Europe. Each afternoon full dark had come earlier, making the cove feel like a hand slowly clenching. Worst of all had been the days of unending rain, the barn and shed and woods dissolving into that grayness. The rain hushed all other sounds, so there wasn't even the call of a cardinal or chatter of a squirrel to let Laurel know she was still in the world. Slidell had dug the grave and afterward reminded her to cover the cabin's one mirror with a dark cloth, as had been done when Laurel's mother died. Even after enough time passed and Laurel could uncover the mirror, she hadn't, unable to shake the dread that she might look in the glass and see no reflection. Not long after the funeral, Slidell came one morning and boarded up the windows. It had felt as if she was being nailed inside the cabin forever.

Walter's steady breaths warmed her neck and she thought of earlier that morning when she dreamed she'd heard her name spoken. The voice had been so real Laurel had opened her eyes and wrapped a quilt around herself to see if someone was outside. She'd fallen back asleep and dreamed that she had taught Walter to speak one word, her name.

When she awoke again the rain had stopped. Walter was up and dressed. Doing it for propriety's sake, just in case Hank came back early. Before too long Hank would be with Carolyn and Walter could share her bed anytime. The thought pleased Laurel, but then curdled at why that was so, and how almost everyone, including Slidell she now realized, had known Hank's plans before she did. By then, she and Walter might be engaged. It was possible, not just a fancy. As Laurel dressed, she imagined ways that Walter could propose—a drawing of them holding hands in church, or shaping a ring out of a gold piece, or even bending a knee with his hand over his heart, like she'd read in a book one time. He'd find a way.

Now that harvesttime was over and she'd picked the last of the beans and corn and grabbled up the last potatoes, she could teach Walter to read and write. All the signs argued a hard winter. Squirrel nests hung in the low branches and the woolly worms bristled, thicker moss on the trees too. There'd be a gracious plenty of snowy days when they could sit by the fire as lines and curves of pencil lead became letters and then words. She'd use the books Miss Calicut had given her, maybe borrow some Appleton's school readers like she'd learned with. Miss Calicut could tell her where to buy a chalk slate and lined paper. She'd be a teacher after all. Laurel smiled at the thought but then another thought came—that Walter able to read and write would make him less needful, maybe change his mind about settling for her. Selfish to think such a thing, a lot of folks would say, and maybe it was, yet she couldn't help it. Turn your mind to the words he'll write you, Laurel told herself, and how those words will bring us closer, and maybe confidence him enough to go to town where it'd be worth the snubs and stares to share an ice cream or let him pick out cloth for a shirt, maybe even dance with her at a victory jubilee.

When Laurel walked to the privy, the chimney smoke wisped downward. Colder weather was coming but not before late afternoon. The trail to the outcrop would be muddy but the rock itself would be dry. She walked back inside.

"I'm fixing us a picnic. There's a place I want to show you."

Laurel folded a quilt in the clothes basket, added a cake tin of cornbread and jar of blackberry jam, last a bottle of muscadine wine. Walter lifted the clothes basket and they walked into the woods. When they came to the two lichened stones, Laurel paused.

"That's where my parents lay."

She and Walter walked into the deeper woods. The rain and wind had felled another dead chestnut and they walked around a trunk so thick neither of them could see over it.

"A blight's killing them," Laurel said. "They claim there won't be a chestnut alive in these mountains before long."

Walter nodded, though whether that meant he already knew she had no idea. Once he could read and write he could tell her so much more, his whole life. It would be like reading chapters in a book, written just for her. The path to the outcrop was slippery so they moved slowly. High above them, the last dark clouds drifted off the edge of the sky. The ground leveled and they came to the wash pool. She set the wine in the water to get cold.

"You'd better look down at the ground. The brightfulness near blinds you at first."

They walked into the light with their heads bowed. Laurel shadowed her eyes with a hand and Walter did the same once he set the basket down. When her eyes adjusted, she took the quilt from the basket and spread it near the ledge. They lay on their backs and let the outcrop's stored heat soak through the cloth and warm them, the only sound water skimming the rock and splashing into the pool below. Bringing Walter here could be a mistake, Laurel suddenly feared, because it brought notice of how dark and dreary the cove was. You can't twine a better-not into every little thing you do with him, Laurel chided herself. Yet how could a woman shut inside a cove all her life know what a man like Walter thought about things, especially since he couldn't talk. Laurel shifted onto a shoulder, their faces almost touching.

"You wouldn't leave without telling me, would you?"

Walter opened his eyes and shook his head.

Laurel moved closer and placed her head on his chest and felt the rise and fall of his breath, the deeper movement of his heart. After a while she went to get the muscadine wine. A trout wavered in the pool's center, its fins orange as fire, flanks spotted red and gold. Spawning colors, but the spawning was done now. Laurel could tell by the trout's tail fin, ragged from fanning sand to cover the eggs. As she took out the bottle, the trout flashed back under the bank.

Laurel returned to the outcrop and opened the cornbread tin and jam jar. She uncorked the bottle and filled the cups. Walter took a swallow and Laurel did too. Its coldness felt good surrounded by the outcrop's warmth. They ate the bread and jam, then drank more wine. After her second cup, the world felt cozied in cotton. Laurel raised up on her elbows and gazed at the far ridge. Except for the black scabs of dead chestnuts, hardwoods quilted the ridge in red and yellow and orange, some purple sweetgum leaves too.

"This," Laurel said, tugging the dress to show the birthmark better. "Does it bother you to look at it?"

Walter shook his head.

"Some folks claim it to mark me as cursed."

Walter moved closer, pulled back the cloth enough to place his lips on the birthmark and kiss it. They lay back down. This is how it'll be, Laurel thought, hours and hours I won't say much and he won't say anything, but he can show me with his eyes and touches that he loves me. He'll play music that's prettier than any words he could say and after I teach him, we can write love letters. Laurel curled an index finger around one of Walter's belt loops and closed her eyes.

When she awoke, the outcrop was half in shadow, the air

cold. Walter was where he had been when she'd fallen asleep, though now his hands were laced behind his head, eyes open. Her finger was still curled in the belt loop and that pleased her. Laurel turned and kissed him, a long lingering kiss, tasting the wine on his breath, letting her hand settle on his cheek.

"We need to go."

As they walked back, the woods were silent and still, the squirrels tucked in their nests, the crows hunched on branches. Like the sky's quick unclouding, all boded frost, maybe a dusting of snow.

Hank returned at dusk, whistling to announce his arrival. He took off his army tunic and hooked it on a peg. He lifted a copy of the *Marshall Sentinel* from the side pocket and set the newspaper by the hearth.

"This week's paper. Mr. Weatherbee gave it to me."

"Oh, good, it's been ever so long since I read one," Laurel said. "I still can't figure why Slidell stopped bringing us his every week."

"Well, I guess at his age you've earned the right to forget a thing or two," Hank answered.

"I reckon so," Laurel said, and handed the coffeepot to Walter. "You can fill the cups while Hank washes up. Then we'll eat."

Afterward, Laurel added applewood to the fire and the three of them pulled chairs close to the hearth. She and Hank shared the newspaper's two sections, Hank spreading the paper on his lap to turn pages better. It was good to have the paper in her hands, not just for the news but as much for the pleasure of reading. Laurel lowered the newspaper and turned to Walter.

"I want to teach you how to read. We'll have lots of time for it once the hard cold comes."

Walter nodded and she turned her gaze to a photograph of a

fifty-pound pumpkin, the farmer embracing it like a huge belly. She read every recipe and every advertisement and every death notice. Hank asked Laurel about several words before they exchanged sections. On the front page there was a picture of Paul Clayton in his uniform, below it an article about his November eighth welcome-home celebration. Below the fold was a picture of an American warship named the *Leviathan*. Laurel showed the pictures to Walter and read the captions, then turned the page and read an article about a skyscraper in New York City that was twenty stories tall. Laurel wished there was a picture so she could ask Walter if he recognized it.

On the newspaper's last page was Chauncey Feith's petition above a long list of names.

"You signed this," Laurel said.

"Feith can be right about one thing," Hank answered. "That professor shouldn't have been talking to them Huns. He's lucky they didn't lock him up too."

Laurel saw other names she knew, including Ansel and Boyce Clayton. At the bottom, separated by a skipped line, were the words *Supporters of This Petition, Mars Hill College Faculty*. Fifteen names followed, all with Professor or Doctor before them.

"Slidell didn't sign it."

"He's just being contrary."

Laurel set the section by the hearth.

"They're saying the war will end soon."

"They were saying that when I was in France," Hank scoffed. "Another month and we'll be home for sure and then it was by Christmas and after that Easter. Maybe it is about done, but how can anyone know? There's never been a fray like this one. I do know one thing though. If that professor's a spy, I'll shed nary a tear if they hang him from that clock tower."

When Laurel turned back to Walter, he was looking at the warship picture, the words beneath it as well. Already trying to start learning, Laurel thought as she went to fetch her sewing basket. She spread the muslin on her lap and guided the cotton thread through the needle.

"It's called the *Leviathan*," Laurel told Walter. "They claim it the biggest ship in the world. You reckon that to be true?"

Walter looked up but made no sign if he believed it or not.

"I'd not misdoubt it," Hank said. "The damn thing weighs fifty-eight thousand tons. That ship would fill up this cove."

Hank fetched his razor and took the whetstone from the mantel. He placed the stone in his right elbow, the razor's blade rasping as Hank's good arm sawed like a fiddler's.

"Would you be of a mind to play some, Walter?" Laurel asked. "It's been near a week and I miss it."

Walter nodded and soon the flute's music filled the room, the rasping of steel on stone heard in the silences. The applewood burned now, adding licks of blue and green to the yellow flames. Laurel's needle caught the fire's light and different colors slid on and off the metal as it dipped and rose, all the while the fire's heat keeping the cold at bay. The Balm of Gilead. That was the pattern she had laid off with the bluing, using her mother's bedspread as her mother had used her mother's. It would be Hank and Carolyn's wedding gift. Laurel paused and pulled another piece of thread over the beeswax, then dipped the needle into the muslin to start another knot. An ashy bottom log buckled, sent up orange sparks, and resettled. Only then did Laurel realize that Walter had quit playing. It was like the flames and the music had so blended that one was lost in the other. She reached for Walter's hand and squeezed it. He laid his other hand on their clasped hands and Laurel saw the scraped knuckles and broken nails, a farmer's hand.

Hank would bring in more kindling before he went to bed, but Laurel rose to do it. She stepped onto the porch and filled her arms. The night embraced her and for once she wanted to be in dark and in cold, because it would be all the better when she went back inside and the fire's warmth and brightness again enveloped her. A few snowflakes came down in a slow windless fall, white and soft as dogwood petals. A tear rolled down her cheek, then another and another, and though Laurel tried to blink them back she couldn't blink fast enough, so set the kindling down and wiped her eyes. The lift of her heart she'd felt on the outcrop she now felt again, and it wasn't just love. She'd felt love before, known its depths when her mother died.

This was something rarer. Happiness, Laurel thought, that must be what this is. She picked up the kindling and went inside. She and Walter and Hank stayed by the hearth past midnight, and no one spoke and no one seemed to want to, as if a single utterance might break some benevolent spell that had been cast over the cabin.

CHAPTER FOURTEEN

Chauncey parked the Model T and crossed the city square, passing Governor Vance's monument before ascending the courthouse steps. He confirmed Senator Zeller's office number in the foyer and walked down the hall, his shoe heels making a solid confident report against the marble floor. He gave the door's wavy glass two firm raps and waited until a woman's voice told him to enter. The room was more austere than he'd imagined, its seating a single long pew and nothing on the walls but a framed photograph of the state capitol. The receptionist sat at a rolltop desk next to the closed inner door of the senator's office. She had a round attractive face and black curly hair, long dark lashes like those of an actress he'd seen in a flicker show. The nameplate said MISS BEATRICE PETTY.

"I have an appointment with Senator Zeller. My name is Chauncey Feith."

"Oh, yes," the woman said, glancing at her calendar. "Sergeant Feith. Just have a seat. The senator will see you soon."

"Thank you," Chauncey said, and sat down.

A newspaper lay on the pew's far end but Chauncey didn't pick it up. He sat knees directly in front of him and back firm against the varnished wood, the manila folder with two copies of the official proclamation in his lap. How long the wait might be he didn't know, which was the reason he hadn't brought the boys along, most of all Jack, who'd been close to insubordinate since the library visit. A state senator was a very busy man and constituents, even important ones, could be left waiting for hours, but the boys might not understand that.

Yet he'd hardly sat down when the inner door opened and Senator Zeller himself invited him in. The senator gave Chauncey a firm handshake and gestured toward the nicest of three chairs opposite the desk, only then seating himself. Senator Zeller asked after his parents and spoke of his affection for Madison County.

"As beautiful a place as there is in North Carolina," Senator Zeller declared, "and its people the salt of the earth. When duty to their country calls, they are ready, which is why I'm honored to be part of the ceremony, even if I have to cede the statehouse to the scalawags and pettifoggers for a day."

"Your presence, sir," Chauncey said, "will mean so much, not just to Paul Clayton but to our whole county."

Senator Zeller leaned back and clasped his hands over his stomach.

"And there was another matter, yes?"

"Yes, sir," Chauncey said, and took out the copies of the proclamation. "I wanted to have one framed to present to Paul Clayton at the ceremony."

Senator Zeller set the copies on his desk and took a pen from his drawer. He signed the bottom line on both, blew the ink dry, and handed them back.

"Thank you, sir," Chauncey said and placed the proclamations back in the folder.

"Thank *you*, Sergeant Feith," Senator Zeller answered, smiling as he came around the desk, set his palm on Chauncey's back as he led him to the door.

"Miss Petty, take a good look at this young man. With his leadership abilities he might one day assume my place in the senate."

Unlike the young librarian at the college, the receptionist's smile was polite and sincere. He wished now he had brought Jack along so the boy could see the respect that Chauncey Feith commanded even in a senator's office.

"It was an honor to meet you, Sergeant Feith," Miss Petty said.

"You as well, Miss Pretty," Chauncey answered.

The instant they left his mouth, Chauncey wanted to grab the words midflight and strangle them. But then Senator Zeller gave a loud chortle and slapped Chauncey on the back.

"What did I tell you, young lady. He even knows how to charm his constituents."

"Yes, sir," Miss Petty said as she demurely lowered her eyes to the calendar.

For a few moments Chauncey stared at the secretary's bowed head, thinking maybe he actually had meant it in a witty but flattering way. He looked up, contemplating a good-bye salute, but Senator Zeller had returned to the inner office.

The sky was overcast as Chauncey descended the courthouse steps, but it felt like the brightest noon. He settled his eyes on Governor Vance's monument until an automobile horn broke his reverie. A limeade would be a fine way to celebrate a good day, but as he walked toward Grant's Pharmacy, Chauncey noticed the two-story brick building with W. O. WOLFE TOMBSTONES AND MONUMENTS painted on the storefront. Shoaled on the wide front porch were slabs and blocks of varying sizes and shapes. By the shop's open door, a huge marble angel hovered over the seeming disarray.

Chauncey turned to the shop's smaller stone wares, some blank but others with chiseled names and dates, on one a cherub whose face, like the angel's, had been vividly rendered. A statue would be raised in Mars Hill when this war ended, the same as after the Revolutionary and Confederate wars. A stone soldier would stand atop it with names on the pedestal inscribed in alphabetical order. Chauncey tried to recall if the earlier statues had mentioned rank. People would see his name on the statue, and that was a pleasing thing, yet it vexed him knowing Tillman Estep's name would be above his. He didn't mind if Paul Clayton or Wesley Ellenburg had names above his, even if they were only privates, but men like Tillman Estep didn't deserve to be on a statue. Their names sullied the others. But there were statues with only one name. Chauncey let his gaze lift from the porch to Governor Vance's monument. Why should he be embarrassed that he'd thought a few times about a political career, especially now that Senator Zeller had suggested that very thing.

Someone coughed inside the shop and a few moments later an old man, tall and gaunt, stooped through the open doorway, his hands and leather apron smudged with white dust.

"W. O. Wolfe, at your service, sir," the stonecutter said, and made a slight bow. "How may I assist you?"

"Do you make monuments of real people?"

"I do," the older man replied, "although, as you can see, more often creatures of the celestial realm."

"And why is that?" Chauncey asked.

"Perhaps they wish an image of what they aspire to be instead of what they are," the stonecutter replied. "The better angels of our nature, corporal as well as spiritual. I can assure you, young squire, from my own humbling experience, that as we grow infirm and life's pleasures pale we long to free ourselves from these sad declining vessels. But enough of such dispiriting parlance. An old man's morbid reckonings are not usually the concerns of youth, nor should they be."

The stonecutter paused, licked the tip of his thumb and rubbed it on his apron, allowed a wan smile.

"And yet, young as you are, you have come to my shop. Noting your uniform and your temperament, might I venture you are soon destined for duty overseas?"

"I didn't say it was for me," Chauncey said.

"Pardon my presumption," the older man answered. "It is indeed my hope that this war will end before you or any others are sent. We have lost too many young men already."

The stonecutter walked over to a partially obscured tablet little larger than a family Bible. He picked up the stone and leaned it against the wall. The old man stared at the tablet with such fixed somberness that Chauncey asked if he'd known the person.

"No, a boy from Leicester. He was killed two weeks ago in France."

The stonecutter stepped back so that Chauncey could see the granite tablet.

"His father said he was one of the first boys in Buncombe County to volunteer."

Beneath the four letters was carved 1892, then a hyphen, a hyphen that hitched Chauncey's own birth date to 1918. Just a coincidence but he felt a shudder and averted his eyes. The old man said something, almost a whisper.

"What?" Chauncey asked.

"The paths of glory lead but to the grave," the stonecutter said. "It's a line from a poem."

"I need to go," Chauncey said. "Thank you for talking to me."

"My pleasure," the stonecutter replied, and spread his palms outward. "As you can see, my companions are less than loquacious, so any conversation is a blessing."

As he followed the French Broad north, Chauncey turned his mind from the gravestone by thinking of a distant time when his visage, like Governor Vance's, might command a statue. Not in Raleigh or Washington necessarily, but perhaps in Mars Hill. He imagined himself white haired and distinguished like Senator Zeller. He and Beatrice, his wife of many years, would arrive on the train for the statue's unveiling. There would be some speeches and proclamations, and of course Chauncey would be expected to make some remarks. He'd mention first the late Senator Franklin Zeller, who had been an early mentor but also introduced Chauncey to Beatrice, and he'd mention Captain Arnold, the man who'd first believed in Chauncey's leadership abilities. Last, he'd call Beatrice to his side and thank her for her support. Beatrice would tell about the first time they'd met and how Chauncey had charmed her with his sense of duty but also his sense of humor, calling her Miss Pretty not Miss Petty. Then Beatrice would turn to the crowd and talk about how Senator Chauncey Feith had dedicated his life to serving his country and there'd be tears on her cheeks as she said that, as this statue attests, everyone now knows Senator Chauncey Feith is a great American, a man of integrity and patriotism and valor, but it was not always the case. Beatrice would explain how the army had needed Sergeant Chauncey Feith on the home front more than they needed him on the front lines in France, where he would have gone without a moment's hesitation and gladly given his life leading men into battle. Then Beatrice would turn to Chauncey and say that the greatest blessing in her life was being married to a man of such nobility and honor. Then they'd have him unveil the statue and the people in Mars Hill would see a figure of Chauncey in his army uniform saluting them, and they'd be inspired, generation after generation, most of all the young men who, when fighting far from home, would remember the statue and the soldier it honored.

As he drove into Mars Hill, Chauncey wished he'd asked the stonecutter which lasted longer, marble or granite.

CHAPTER FIFTEEN

As the men lingered over their morning coffee, Laurel finished the pumpkin pie they'd have for dessert come evening. She pinched the dough around the pie plate's edges, stippled the dough with a fork as she added sugar.

"You mind getting the cinnamon for me, Hank?"

Hank was about to rise but Walter motioned for him to stay seated. Walter took the cinnamon tin from the shelf and handed it to her. She sprinkled cinnamon over the dough and set the tin beside her. Only when the men left and she was placing the tin back on the shelf did Laurel realize.

She sat down at the table and tried to remember another time she'd used the cinnamon while Walter watched her. She couldn't remember one and even if there had been the shelf held a dozen tins the same size and shape. Laurel pondered if hearing such a long word had helped him, but Walter had known right away that it wasn't a tin labeled sassafras or pennyroyal. She got up and stood in front of the shelf. As she searched for some difference that might explain it, other things perched in her mind—like Walter looking so carefully at the newspaper's words and the time in bed she'd heard her name and thought it a dream, or how he'd used a pencil so familiar like, even how the words *cinnamon* and *Vaterland* looked similar.

You could have just forgot a time when he saw you use it, Laurel told herself. Besides, why would he pretend things that just made his life harder. Laurel got up and finished the pie and set it in the stove. Soon the smell of pie filled the cabin, usually a soothing thing, but not today.

After they'd finished noon-dinner, Laurel told Hank she was going to go spruce up Slidell's house. If you get hungry before I'm back, there's beans and potatoes, she said, waited until the men were almost to the door before telling Walter she needed his help for a minute.

"I'll meet you outside," Hank said.

Laurel pointed at the flour barrel, which easily weighed a hundred pounds.

"I need you to move it closer to the larder."

As Walter lifted the barrel he gave a soft grunt. A grunt, not a puff of breath. Laurel dared not meet his eyes, instead looked toward the door. Hank had set the shotgun back by the door weeks ago. Laurel's heart hammered against her chest as Walter crossed the room and passed within a stretched arm of the weapon.

She waited until she heard the men working before unbuckling the shotgun and prying out the shell. Laurel placed it and the extra shells in Hank's closet under her pillow and left. Slidell was in his field cutting cabbage but Laurel didn't pause to speak or ask to borrow the wagon. She needed to walk, to have something to do besides fret. Leaves rasped and acorns popped beneath her feet as she made her way down to the pike. What it all meant was a knot she couldn't unsnarl, but when it did unsnarl, what then? Laurel remembered a story Slidell had told her father. One winter day Slidell and Ginny had pulled up a big oak stump in his pasture and beneath it was a good half hundred rattlers and copperheads knotted in a big ball. There was snow on the ground and Slidell said those dark bodies pulled apart and began crawling over the whiteness and it looked like he'd opened a crack in hell itself.

When Laurel got to Mars Hill, she went straight to the schoolhouse and waited on a hall bench. She smelled the chalk dust and linseed oil. Even if she were blind, Laurel would know where she was. But there had been changes. Electric wires vined the walls and there was another classroom added on the back. Laurel listened as both teachers asked and answered questions. As it got closer to two o'clock, the students fidgeted in their chairs and whispered to each other, restless as bees in a bee box.

The college's bell rang twice and students poured into the halls with their book satchels, the town boys and girls toting their brown paper bags and lunch boxes, the country children with their milk pails. A teacher Laurel had never seen before stood at her door, telling the students not to run. When the last child left Miss Calicut's class, Laurel stepped in the doorway. Miss Calicut was erasing the chalkboard. Laurel remembered how she'd sometimes gone outside after school and clapped the erasers together, holding them like cymbals as she raised yellow clouds that had made her cough. She looked around the classroom and saw the same colorful globe beside Miss Calicut's desk and the same big map of the United States. But now there was also a poster that said BUY WAR BONDS and beside it a painting of a Carolina Parakeet, a real painting, not a copy. The biggest change was how the desks and the room itself were so much smaller. Laurel remembered how even in her last year her feet had barely touched the floor.

"Is it hard to believe you ever fit inside one of those desks?" Miss Calicut asked.

Laurel looked up and saw Miss Calicut had turned her way.

"Yes, ma'am. It is."

"It's probably even harder to imagine an old woman like me could have ever been that small."

"You don't seem old."

Miss Calicut smiled.

"Kind of you to say so, Laurel. That's one of the best things about teaching. Being around children does make a part of me still feel young, even with my gray hair. But look at you, pretty as a bluebird."

Laurel blushed.

"It's the truth, Laurel Shelton, you were always pretty and smart to boot, and brave, you and your brother both. Speaking of which, I've heard Hank's back from the war. That must be a blessing for you."

"Yes, ma'am. He and Carolyn Weatherbee are going to get married soon."

"They'll make a good match," Miss Calicut said. "Carolyn was a good student, though not as good as you. How about Marcie Bettingfield? Do you see her much?"

"Just at the victory jubilees."

"She was a good friend to you, I remember that."

"Yes, ma'am."

"Here I've been nattering on and hardly given you a chance to speak," Miss Calicut said. "Is there something I can do for you, or did you just come to brighten my day by visiting?"

"I need to ask about a word, the meaning of it."

"What word?"

"I'm not sure how to say it."

Miss Calicut handed Laurel a pencil and piece of paper.

"*Vaterland*," Miss Calicut said. "I've never seen that word before. Did you look it up in the dictionary I gave you?"

"It wasn't in there."

"Let's look in mine."

Miss Calicut pulled a dictionary from the wooden shelf above the fire grate. She turned to the *V*'s and let her index finger slide down the page.

"It's not in mine either. Where'd you see the word?"

"It was on a sort of medal."

"Any other words on it?"

"No."

"Was the word capitalized?" Miss Calicut asked. "It could be a last name or a place."

"I couldn't tell. The letters looked the same size."

"It could be a foreign word, but it's not Latin or French sounding. Are you needing to get back home quick?"

"No, ma'am."

"If we can find him, I think I know someone who can tell us," Miss Calicut said. "Just give me a minute to tidy up."

Laurel crossed the room to see the parakeet better.

"An art student at the college painted that for me," Miss Calicut said. "I thought my students ought to know such a pretty bird once lived in these mountains."

"I saw a few last winter," Laurel said.

"Last winter?" Miss Calicut asked. "There was an article in the Asheville paper that claimed there were none left."

"It looked to be five or six."

"I'm glad to hear that," Miss Calicut said. "Something that pretty needs to be in the world, don't you think?"

Laurel nodded as Miss Calicut stepped from behind her desk.

"I'm ready," Miss Calicut said. "We'll try his office at the college first."

They walked along Main Street and then through the arch and up the hill. Miss Calicut had brought Laurel's class to the college on a field trip once, and like the classroom chairs, the campus was smaller than Laurel remembered, but the college was still a wonder with its wide green lawn and bell tower and whole buildings where all a person did was learn about things. If it had just been about having the smarts, I could have gone to school here, Laurel told herself, and a bitterness not felt in years overcame her.

"There," Miss Calicut said, and pointed to a brick building with ARTS AND SCIENCES chiseled on its gable. "I don't know if Professor Mayer's in his office, but we can at least see."

They entered the building and walked down the hallway, the fresh-polished floors shining dully. They passed several offices, including one with a name on the door Laurel recognized from the petition. Miss Calicut raised her hand to her mouth as they stood before the last door, its pebbled-glass window shattered. On the wood beneath, HUN was printed in slashes of red paint.

"I didn't know it had gotten this bad for him," Miss Calicut said.

"What do you mean?" Laurel asked.

"Professor Mayer teaches foreign languages, including German, and there have been rumors that he's some sort of spy. It's ridiculous, of course. The poor man is in his seventies. He's kind and generous and no more a spy than I am."

An office door up the hall opened and a man in a coat and tie stared at them.

"Come on," Miss Calicut told Laurel. "I know where he lives."

They walked back through town and followed Lee Street past Miss Calicut's boardinghouse and down another block.

"To be treated so badly because of a few foolish people," Miss Calicut sighed, "but you've had plenty of experience with that, haven't you."

"Yes, ma'am."

They came to a small white house whose windows were curtained. Miss Calicut knocked on the door.

"He doesn't hear well," Miss Calicut said, and rapped the wood harder. "Professor Mayer?"

A hand peeled back a curtain edge, but the door did not open.

"Who is it?" a muffled voice answered.

"Amanda Calicut."

"Who?"

"Amanda Calicut. You taught me Latin years ago. I teach at the elementary school."

The brass knob turned and the door slowly opened. A man in a rumpled suit and bow tie stood before them, his hand on the knob as if he might yet close the door. He was no taller than Laurel, rosy cheeked and white haired. Around his head was a metal band, on one end an earpiece. A wire attached the band to a gadget clipped on his shirt.

"We're sorry to bother you, Professor," Miss Calicut said. "We just had a question about something. But if you don't want visitors . . ."

Professor Mayer took his hand off the doorknob.

"No, do come in. I didn't mean to be rude, but there have been some incidents of late."

"I know," Miss Calicut said, "and like I told Laurel, it's a disgrace."

"Please," Professor Mayer said, and nodded at a settee.

He shuffled across the room and sat down in a leather armchair. A Windsor chair, that's what it was called, Laurel knew, though she'd only seen one in the wish book. The room smelled of tobacco and the wintergreen salve she'd rubbed on her father's skin those last years. A bookshelf covered a whole wall, more volumes than Laurel had ever seen except in a library. Professor Mayer turned a small knob on his hearing machine.

"I can't offer you much as far as refreshment," Professor Mayer said. "I don't expect many visitors these days."

"We're fine," Miss Calicut answered, and rose from the settee, handed Professor Mayer the paper. "Do you know what this word means?"

Professor Mayer quickly gave it back and glanced toward the door.

"Did somebody send you?"

"No, sir," Miss Calicut answered. "I mean, Laurel asked me, but she didn't send me to you. I just thought you might know."

"Perhaps it's best if you leave now," Professor Mayer said, and rose from the chair.

"It was on a medallion I saw," Laurel said. "I just want to know what it means."

Professor Mayer did not sit back down, but he didn't shuffle toward the door either.

"This medallion, did you get it at the internment camp in Hot Springs?"

"So it is German," Miss Calicut said. "I knew it wasn't a romance language."

"I didn't get it up there," Laurel said. "I found it."

"Where?" Miss Calicut asked.

Laurel hesitated.

"Near the river, on the bank."

"The German prisoner who escaped," Miss Calicut said. "Do you think it belonged to him?"

Professor Mayer's eyes remained on Laurel. Still suspicious, she could tell, but also curious.

"When you found the medallion," he asked, "was anyone nearby?"

"No, sir."

"The word," Miss Calicut asked. "What does it mean?"

Professor Mayer raised a hand to his forehead as if to confirm a fever. He took the hand away and grimaced.

"What Chauncey Feith and those others are claiming, I know it's not true," Miss Calicut said. "Laurel and I both would never do or say anything to harm you."

"It means fatherland," Professor Mayer said.

"Fartherland?" Laurel asked.

"No," Professor Mayer said, and pronounced the word more slowly. "It's also the name of a German ocean liner, one that got stranded in New York Harbor in 1914. When we entered the war, part of the crew was sent to Hot Springs."

"Of course," Miss Calicut said. "I knew all that. I'd forgotten the ship's name."

"Why didn't it sail back to Germany?" Laurel asked.

"The French or British would have sunk it," Professor Mayer said.

"What did they do?" Laurel asked. "I mean those three years."

"Almost anything they pleased," Professor Mayer answered. "Ruser, the commodore, told me he went to museums and symphonies, even banquets. Then in 1917 the ship was seized and the men declared enemy aliens."

Laurel grew dizzy for a few moments, the room tilting slightly before leveling again. She had walked three miles and hadn't eaten since breakfast, but that wasn't the cause. There was too much to try and understand. It was like stepping into what looked like a shallow stream and suddenly being underwater with a suckhole pulling her deeper.

"Are you all right, Laurel?" Miss Calicut asked.

"Yes, ma'am," Laurel said.

"Let me get you some water, child," the professor said.

He left the room and returned with a filled glass. Laurel took a swallow, then another.

"I suspect you've heard more than enough so we can go," Miss Calicut said.

"No, ma'am, I want to hear more, I really do," Laurel said, setting the empty glass beside the settee. "So the *Vaterland* wasn't a ship for a war but like the *Titanic*?"

"More impressive than the *Titanic*," Professor Mayer said. "When I was up at Hot Springs last April, the men swore the *Vaterland* made the *Titanic* look like a river barge. Prussian bombast, I assumed, but then I did some research. It *is* the largest ship ever built, and Pompeiian in its extravagance–silk curtains, marble washstands, gold cutlery, even bath pools and a wintergarden. But no more. What wasn't plundered was thrown overboard."

Professor Mayer went to the shelf and took out a book, withdrew a yellowing newspaper article and handed it to Miss Calicut.

"I probably should get rid of it. If found here it would only cause further suspicion," Professor Mayer said, and sat back down. He closed his eyes a moment, let out a sigh as he opened them. "This whole matter is so ironic. I was initially summoned to Hot Springs to read postcards and letters, to make sure the internees were *not* spies."

"Read it along with me, Laurel," Miss Calicut said, and held it between them.

Below a photograph of the ocean liner was a caption.

War Charity Fete on the *Vaterland*
Giant Hamburg-American Liner
Houses a Fancy Dress
Festival
To Aid Central Powers

"They were raising money for Germany, not us," Miss Calicut exclaimed.

"Look at the date," Professor Mayer said. "Nevertheless, I understand Mr. Hearst has had cause to regret his presence there."

"The *Vaterland*'s a troop ship now, isn't it?" Laurel asked.

"Yes," Professor Mayer said. "It's called the *Leviathan*."

"I knew that too," Laurel said. "It was in the *Marshall Sentinel* a while back."

For a few moments they were all silent. Laurel looked around the room. Next to the bookshelves was a painting of a blue sky above green hills, but the curtains shut out so much light the painting was drab as the bookshelves. It seemed a shame that the curtains were closed.

"The medallion," Laurel asked. "You think it belonged to a German who escaped?"

"It's certainly possible," Professor Mayer said.

"Didn't they think he got away on a train?" Miss Calicut asked.

"They presumed so," Professor Mayer answered. "The boat he stole was found below the trestle. A mill worker later claimed to have encountered him, but the search dogs couldn't pick up a trail. Of course, someone could have caught him and decided to exact his own justice. Such things have occurred. American citizens have been hanged by mobs, just because they spoke German."

"If somehow he was still around and he got caught, do you think people might do that to him?" Laurel asked. "I mean, if I happened to see him, would it be better not to say anything?"

"Of course not," Professor Mayer said, "a man in such desperate straits is capable of anything, including killing, to protect himself."

"Professor Mayer's right," Miss Calicut said. "You have no cause to think he's still around, do you?"

"No, ma'am," Laurel answered.

"After two months, he's surely far away," Professor Mayer said.

"Surely," Miss Calicut agreed.

"This medallion, what did you do with it?" Professor Mayer asked.

"I hid it."

"Keep it hidden, child," Professor Mayer said. "Were someone to see it there could be serious trouble for you. *Libenter homines id quad volunt credunt.*"

"Men are glad to believe that which they wish for?" Miss Calicut asked.

Professor Mayer smiled for the first time.

"Well done. I'm glad you took my Latin class and not my German. No doubt Chauncey Feith and his minions would accuse you of teaching the children to be spies. It is best to keep what we have discussed among ourselves."

"I won't tell anyone," Miss Calicut replied.

"I won't either," Laurel said. "But that article. If you aren't of a mind to keep it, I'd like to have it. I'll keep it hid with the medallion."

"I don't believe that would be wise," Professor Mayer answered. "If someone found out I gave it to you . . ."

"I'd not tell them, I promise. I'd say I'd found the article and the medallion together."

Professor Mayer hesitated a few moments longer.

"Please," Laurel said.

"All right," he sighed. "But show it to no one else, at least not until this war is over."

Miss Calicut stood and Laurel did as well.

"Thank you for your time, Professor," Miss Calicut said.

"Yes, thank you," Laurel said.

"Well," Miss Calicut said as they stepped off the porch, "we've had quite an afternoon."

"Yes, ma'am," Laurel said.

They walked back up Lee Street until they stood in front of Mrs. Jarvis's boardinghouse.

"Want to come in for tea and a piece of sweet bread?"

"Thank you, but no," Laurel said. "I need to get back to the cove."

Miss Calicut took her hand.

"Think about finishing school, Laurel. It's not too late. Even if you can't teach around here because of some ignorant folks, there are other places."

"Yes, ma'am," Laurel said. "Thank you for helping me, and not just today."

Miss Calicut went inside and Laurel checked the clock tower. Both hands were on the three, pointing west toward the cove. She couldn't shake the notion that the hands being locked like that was some kind of omen. It could be two hands clasped or two hands bound. There'd be a telephone in the boardinghouse and she could have Miss Calicut call the high sheriff in Marshall, or Laurel could walk all the way to the county courthouse and find the high sheriff herself. That way no mob would get hold of him.

Capable of anything, Professor Mayer had said, but Walter could have killed her and Hank while they slept, or stolen what little they had and gone on. He hadn't come to the cabin on his own or asked to stay. Laurel had brought him and Hank had given him a job. He'd have never come off the ridge otherwise.

But he had stayed, eaten their food and slept in their bed. They'd trusted him with their very lives but he'd not trusted them, even after he and Laurel had laid down together. Even after that. Laurel thought of the morning she'd heard him speak but believed it a dream. But the dream was thinking a man with no cause to do so would wander into the cove and want to stay there with her. How could she have ever believed such a thing for a minute, much less this long? And yet, he had come back when he could have left on the train, and the one word he had said, of all the words in German or English, had been her name.

Laurel passed the last storefront and soon only trees lined the pike. If she did go straight back to the cove, what about Hank, who'd told Michael Davenport he wished he could kill a dozen Germans for what they'd done. And the German who'd pretended to be wounded, tricking Hank with words, pretending to be English. She'd have to explain that the men at Hot

Springs weren't soldiers at all, never had been, but that might not matter to Hank. He might turn Walter in anyway, or worse. It would be safer to tell Hank after the war ended. If Walter was still around. Maybe all he'd wanted was a place so lonesome no one would know him a German until it no longer mattered. Then he could return to New York or Germany or wherever he wanted, alone. Perhaps he had been willing to do everything possible to stay in the safety of the cove, even lay down with Laurel.

The ghostlike feeling she'd had last October came upon her again, so she watched for anything that would anchor her to the world—the feel of her feet on the pike, the chuffing of a woodcock, what shadow she might cast, most of all for what waited until now to show its brightness—the scarlet sumac and yellow clumps of sneezeweed, purple galax, and, as she crossed over a spring flow, the silver bark of a beech tree. She passed a last field where orange pumpkins squatted, close by a haystack golden in the afternoon sun. Laurel touched the newspaper article in her pocket, something else real. She stopped and took it out, read it again in hopes something might be in it to help her know what to do.

> The giant Hamburg-American liner *Vaterland*, which has been resting quietly alongside her pier in Hoboken since the beginning of the war, was ablaze with lights last night above and below deck when the ship was thrown open to the public for a concert and festival in aid of the war charities of the Central Powers. It is expected that $7,000 will be added to the fund by the fete.
>
> The big courtyard was filled with automo-

biles and the pier was decorated with colored lights and flags in honor of the occasion. Employees of the steamship line, dressed in fancy costumes, met the guests at the entrance and drove them on electric trolleys to the gangway.

Six hundred and fifty or more members of the German-American colony in New York and their friends paid $10 a ticket for admission and bought all kinds of souvenirs on board to aid the fund. After the supper served in the grand dining saloon there was a concert in the music room under the direction of Otto Goritz of the Metropolitan Opera Company, a cabaret show in the drawing room on the sun deck, dancing in the ballroom and all kinds of other entertainments to amuse the guests.

The women and many of the men wore fancy costumes and all appeared to enjoy the fun which had been provided for them. A portion of the starboard side of the upper promenade deck was fitted up with flowers and flags, where pictures of a tour through Palestine were shown, accompanied by orchestral music, including harps, and was labeled "In Heaven."

The crowd filled the other place opposite on the port side, which was decorated with scenery, depicting the infernal regions, artistically constructed by the crew of the *Vaterland* and filled with small tables, where waiters dressed as imps staggered to and fro carrying trays laden with glasses of cheering beverages.

> Commodore Hans Ruser sat at a table surrounded with a bevy of fair women, and appeared, for the time, to have forgotten the war was on. Vice-directors Julious P. Meyer and William G. Siskel of the Hamburg-American Line, who gave the use of the liner for the fete, were present to support the Commodore.
>
> Among those who were on the list were Mr. and Mrs. William Randolph Hearst; Hy Mayer, the cartoonist; Major Hans Tauscher; Jacques Urius, the German tenor from the Metropolitan Opera House, and many others well known in the social and professional world. The officers and crew of the *Vaterland* were all dressed in muster uniforms, and it was expected that the last of the guests would leave the Hamburg-American Line pier this morning as the Hoboken milkman is going his round.

Laurel folded the article and placed it in her dress pocket. Her father's bad heart, her mother's infected thumb, Hank's conscription. They'd happened and she'd had no say in any of it. But she did choose to bring Walter to the cabin and to lay down with him, and now, another choice. Preacher Goins claimed at her father's funeral that all things human had been decided before God created the world, but Laurel didn't want to believe that. She could turn around and walk back this very moment to town. Or she could pretend she didn't know who Walter really was or tell him to his face she did know. But choose wrong and she would live out the rest of her life knowing it might have been otherwise.

When Laurel came to where she could turn off the pike or head on to Marshall, she went up the wayfare a few yards and sat on a log. What if Chauncey Feith was right, that the men in the camp were spies and Professor Mayer was one too? There was the newspaper article, but couldn't that be made up, just a trick to make folks think the *Vaterland* hadn't had a bunch of spies on it? She read the article again. Like something out of a fairy tale, and couldn't that be simply because it was? But the print and paper looked real, and in the upper corner the words *New York Times* and a page number, same as the *Marshall Sentinel*. Laurel placed the article back in her pocket.

An acorn lay at her feet and she picked it up, settled its roundness between her finger and thumb. She thought again of how Walter could have gotten on the train that morning when Slidell took him to town, left once and for all. Yet he'd come back to the cove, come back to her.

She had blinded herself before by expecting the best, first with Hank and Carolyn and now with Walter, when her whole life had taught her to expect the worst. If you can't believe some good things can happen in your life, how else can you go on? Laurel thought, but now she'd let herself ponder only the bad outcomes of what she'd learned, then decide which would be the worst one. She rubbed the acorn, feeling its smoothness but also its solidity. The woods were very quiet, no breeze to stir the leaves. A wagon passed on the pike, a whole family from the sound of the voices.

The woods had begun to get shadowy by the time Laurel dropped the acorn and stood up, brushed the back of her dress, and walked on up the wayfare. You'll have to live with what you've decided the rest of your life, Laurel told herself, and if Miss Calicut and Professor Mayer are right, that might not be very long. But dying, even if it was today, wasn't the worst. Being alone in the cove, like last winter, that would be the worst thing. Dead and still in the world was worse than dead and in the ground. Dead in the ground at least gave you the hope of heaven.

As Laurel approached Slidell's house, she suddenly remembered the boar hog. She'd walked right past where Slidell had seen it again last month, even got a shot at it. Maybe there was only so much scared a body could hold. Laurel didn't stop to speak to Slidell. She passed under the ash limb and its bottles and tin scraps, feeling the spills of salt and the broken glass beneath her feet. The path slanted downward and the shadows deepened. She felt like she was wading into dark water, with little in the gloaming to anchor her to the world. Then she heard the flute, faint and far off, a sound she'd followed up the creek to its source three months ago and followed the night she and Walter first laid down together. Follow it a while longer, Laurel told herself.

CHAPTER SIXTEEN

"We were of a mind to wait for you," Hank said when Laurel stepped on the porch, "so I asked Walter to play some tunes while we did."

"That was kindly of you," Laurel said.

When he put the flute in its case and stood, she turned away. I'll not be able to hide the knowing from him, Laurel told herself, not even one evening.

"Let's eat then," she said. "I need to gather some mint before it's full dark."

After supper Laurel didn't bother with washing the dishes or putting things up, just said she'd like some company. She got an egg basket and they walked into the woods, the leaves thick and rustling at their feet, the branches above black and stark. She didn't speak.

When they got to the creek, Laurel set the basket on the bank. Even if Hank heard a scream, he'd not get here in time. She wouldn't scream though, or even try to get away. She'd just let it be over and done with. Walter crouched and began picking mint leaves as Laurel stood behind him and let the words gather inside her, each finding its proper place. She pictured every letter's curves and lines to make the words more solid and real. When Laurel had her sentence, she spoke.

"The reason you pretend you can't talk is because you're German, isn't it?"

He slowly dropped the mint he'd gathered into the basket. His eyes were on the creek, maybe gauging its depth before splashing across and running on into the woods, or searching for a rock big enough to fill his hand.

First came a cough, then a clearing of the throat followed by a raspy *yes* before a bout of coughing as he turned to face her.

"Some people say you could be a spy."

"A musician," he said, clearing his throat with each few words. "Not a spy."

"The professor I talked to today claimed you weren't a spy," Laurel said. "He told me about the camp up at Hot Springs."

He still crouched, his left hand on the ground to better steady himself.

"Will he turn me in?"

"He doesn't know you're in the cove," Laurel said. "He just knows you escaped."

"And you," he said, his free hand rubbing his throat as if to coax the words out. "Will you turn me in?"

"If I was I'd have already done it."

He stood up and Laurel handed the newspaper clipping to him.

"I know you can read it."

He studied the article for a few moments and handed it back.

"What's your name," Laurel asked, "your real name?"

"Jurgin Walter Koch."

"You thought I'd turn you in if you told me, even after I'd laid down with you?"

"No, not you."

He was not whispering now, and she heard the accent through the raspiness and throat clearings.

"You think Hank would turn you in?"

"You think not?"

"I don't know."

"I could not take the risk."

For a moment, it was as if, after a few dozen words, they had run out of things to say. The creek was low and muted, nothing like in spring or after a summer thunderstorm. Soon there'd be days cauls of ice silenced the creek completely. Trout would be locked beneath the ice, hardly moving.

"Tell me your real name again," Laurel said. "I want to be able to say it right."

"Walter is my real name, and just that name is better for now."

"How did you learn English?"

"Some at the conservatory, then on the *Vaterland* since half the passengers spoke English. Most I learned in New York. Off the ship, speaking German, especially my last year there, could be dangerous."

"The conservatory," Laurel asked. "Is that where you learned to play music?"

"Yes, in Leipzig. I went there at age twelve."

"Did your parents send you?"

"They were farmers. I was a *stipendiat*, so my parents did not have to give money."

"So that's how you learned to do farmwork," Laurel said. "How come you were on the *Vaterland*?"

"My teacher at the conservatory arranged it. He saw the war coming and decided I'd be safer in the ship's orchestra. It was not a thing I wished to do, but he said I owed it to him, that he had made too many efforts for me to become war fodder."

"Did you want to get back to Germany when you escaped?"

"No, New York. I thought I could be safe there."

Laurel looked into his eyes and was reminded of the first time she'd seen them. The same blue as a river pool, but also that same sort of depth.

"Which is why you've stayed here. To be safe, I mean?"

"At the first, not now," Walter said, his hand reaching for hers.

Laurel hesitated, then placed her palm against his as she spoke.

"They say the war is almost over."

"I hope so."

For a few moments they held hands, their eyes not on each other but looking at the creek. The water was so clear that even in the waning light Laurel could see a rhododendron leaf slowly drifting over the pool's sandy bottom. Know everything now, she decided, right now once and forever. She tried again to summon the right words, then turned to him.

"When the war is over, you will still want to be with me?"

Walter did not reply at first. It was as if he'd waited until this moment to decide. Don't look away, Laurel told herself. When he answers, make him look you in the eye so you'll know it's certain true.

"Yes," Walter said. "Yet what about Hank?"

"We won't let him know until after the war's over. Then what I do is not Hank's concerning. He never asked me about his plans."

Laurel moved closer and took his free hand.

"I'll leave right now if you want me to. I'll go with you to New York or Germany or anywhere else."

"Traveling now is too dangerous," Walter replied.

"Then we'll wait for the war to end," Laurel said. "Where will we go?"

"To New York. Before I was arrested, a man named Goritz offered me an audition."

"He's the conductor in the newspaper article."

Walter nodded.

"We'll go to New York then," Laurel said.

A soft crunching of leaves came from the ridge.

"It's nothing but a squirrel or turkey," Laurel said, but she felt Walter's hands tense.

"We mustn't speak anywhere near the cabin."

"I don't think I can stand that," Laurel said. "I mean, we could whisper, if Hank was outside and us inside."

Walter let go of her hands and took a step back.

"No, we will not risk that," he said, the harshness of his tone surprising her. "The newspaper article, give it to me."

Laurel handed it to him. He shredded the article and threw it in the water. They watched the pieces grow soggy and then sink.

"The newspaper made it all seem so magical," Laurel said.

"I have come to believe it was," Walter said.

"And yet, real too."

"Yes," Walter said.

"I can't imagine such a thing, much less believe such a thing could be," Laurel said. "But if you tell me everything about the ship maybe I can."

"Now?"

"Yes."

"My voice won't last so long."

"Tell me about one part of it then," Laurel said, "your favorite part."

Walter was silent for several moments. She could tell that he was forming a picture of the ship, or part of it, in his mind.

"The orchestra performed on the B deck," Walter said, "so I'll tell you of it."

"Everything you can remember," Laurel said.

As he spoke she stopped him to ask about a term or describe something more slowly so she could see it in her own head, remember it better.

"Tell it to me again," Laurel told him when he'd finished. "And if there's something you left out make sure you put it in. I want to know it every bit as good as you do. That way it's part of me, and this place can't lay claim on me any more, not really, even if the war never ended."

Walter took a long breath and exhaled. He began again, added a few more details. When he finished, Laurel asked who'd done the oil paintings but he didn't know.

"We had better go back," Walter said, "while there remains light."

"I know," Laurel said, "but let's stay just a while longer. I've got so many questions but it's not only that. I need a few minutes to let myself know all of this is real."

IV

CHAPTER SEVENTEEN

"You ever dug a well?" Hank asked on Friday morning.

Walter shook his head and Hank gave a wan smile.

"You're going to find out why we cut firewood and boarded windows first. I figured if there's a chore to run a man off it's likely this one."

They went to the shed and once inside shouldered themselves into the sledge's leather harnesses. The runners had sunk into the dirt floor so they heaved at the same moment to free them. Once they got the sledge outside, they paused to catch their breath. Laurel was at the old well and Walter saw the curve of her breast as she reached for the bucket. A languorous yearning overcame him as he recalled that breast cupped in his hand last Sunday morning. Afterward, Laurel had risen from the bed, turning her back to him as she put her gown on. There had been an inexplicable sadness in that, not the turning away, but seeing the white and purple skin, its beauty and smoothness, hidden again.

"A horse would sure make this easier," Hank said, "but I figure we can get it up to the cliff and back."

They dragged the sledge past the cabin and the cornfield where the scarecrow stood amid the wrack of graying cornstalks. They followed the fence line and entered the cliff's densest shadow. Rocks and boulders thickened, soon too many to navigate. Whether from fallen stone or lack of light, no trees grew here, only scabs of grass. Hank picked up a rock the size and shape of a dinner plate.

"Ones like this is what we're needing," he said, and dropped the rock into the sledge.

They wandered amid the rocks and boulders, gathering suitable ones. More than any time before, Walter was aware of the cliff's magnitude. He had seen icebergs almost as huge, but the granite's solidity was something that could not be breeched by a hull or softened by the sun, so solid it appeared capable of outlasting time itself. When the sledge was three-quarters full, Hank raised his hand.

"That's enough. We just need to rock the walls three foot high."

The trip back was more jerks and stops than a steady drag. When they finally got the sledge beside the new well, sweat beaded their brows despite the cool weather. Hank took out his handkerchief and wiped his face. He motioned Walter closer to the well so they both could stare into its black void.

"This is as onerous a chore as I know and it's two spades to a pair of clubs which is worse, hauling that barrel up or being the fellow who fills it. But I do know it's more dangerous being in the hole. If that rope snaps when you're going up or down, you'll be getting off light with a broke leg. If it happens when the barrel's coming up, you'll likely be graveyard dead, because there's nowhere to dodge and it'll stove in your head. You don't want nothing, I mean nothing, falling in a hole when it's that deep. A fellow over at Antioch dropped a hammer and it killed the digger. And that's just one thing to fret over. Your walls can cave in if they ain't plumb, especially if you hit sand, and the air can get gassy on you, which is why you got to work without a lantern. What I'm saying is we need to be damn careful, whether we're the one up or down."

Hank paused.

"Have I scared you off it?"

Walter shook his head as he studied the wooden windlass and staved oak barrel, most of all the rope that linked them. Set inside the barrel was a shovel, its handle no longer than a piece of firewood.

"Come winter, you'll be glad we put up with this aggravation, especially when you don't have to send that bucket down halfway to China to draw water."

Hank nodded at the hole.

"Want me to go first?"

Walter shook his head.

"All right," Hank said, and positioned himself by the winch handle. "Put your feet in the barrel and it'll make it easy on your arms. When you get to the bottom, tug the rope and I'll know to raise some so you can dig. Tug on it again when you got a load. I'll spell you midmorning."

Walter grabbed the rope with both hands and set his feet in

the barrel. He leaned back until his head cleared the windlass. The winch creaked and he descended, the cove's shallow light only a narrowing circle above. Soon he could not see the walls or hear the winch. The air moistened and smelled of earth. The barrel kept descending. He looked up and the opening was no bigger than a silver dollar. The barrel finally bumped not earth but a cairn of rock left from the dynamiting. Walter got out and looked up at the coin of light. He tugged the rope and the bucket rose level with his chest.

He wedged himself against the dirt wall and began filling the barrel with the blasted rocks, working solely by feel. He chunked a last rock in the barrel and tugged the rope and the barrel rose, his hands on its wooden sides, leveling the ascent. Shovel in hand, Walter stabbed the soil loose around the last dynamited stones and tried to turn his mind to something other than unraveling ropes and crumbling walls.

He thought of Goritz and how after the charity concert the conductor had sought him out and asked where Walter had studied. When he answered Leipzig with Herr Schuler, Goritz nodded approvingly. Your talent is being wasted, Goritz had said. I will audition you and if it goes well I can, if you wish, get you United States citizenship. You are not quite ready yet, though. For the next six months, practice until your arms ache and your lips bleed. The suffering will be good for you. A slight smile had crossed the conductor's face. If you haven't already found a woman who will break your heart, find one. What we played tonight, especially the Mozart, requires suffering.

April sixth. He'd marked the audition date on his calendar, but as winter moved into spring rumors of an American declaration of war were rampant. Off the *Vaterland*, he spoke as little as possible. Commodore Ruser made no pronouncements but most onboard believed they would be forced to sail for Europe. Men spoke of the *Lusitania* and presumed the *Vaterland*'s chance of survival no better. That last evening as Walter walked back to make curfew, there were more indications of a coming war. The window of Heinaman's Shoe Repair had been shattered. Men passed a whiskey bottle outside Schuman's Hoffbrau House and bellowed about traitors. A man set fire to a poster advertising Pabst Blue Ribbon beer. Walter thought about going to Goritz right then, but the flute and all his savings were on the ship. He went on, passing a drunk searching for a recruitment office, a stevedore lingering on a church step, a thumbprint of ash smudged on his forehead. He was already on the dock when he saw the American flag on the *Vaterland*'s masthead, the pier and deck crowded with soldiers and policemen. He turned to flee, but he'd been seen. He was caught and shoved into the back of a police wagon, taken to a Bowery jail.

The barrel eclipsed the well mouth's center, leaving only a rind of light. The barrel descended and Walter threw in the last dynamited rocks, picked up the shovel and began digging as best he could in such narrow quarters. He tugged the rope and the filled barrel rose. The darkness dimmed slightly and Walter looked up. The well mouth was clear and the air around him felt less constricted. He leaned against the earthen wall, felt its dampness on his back. The barrel reappeared, swaying on its rope above him.

He had seen the dead man on the way to North Carolina. When the train stopped at a crossroads in Virginia named Damascus, he and his forty-nine shipmates stretched and smoked on the depot's platform. No handcuffs bound their wrists but the guards had shotguns and billy clubs at the ready. As the men were herded back onto the train, one of the guards said a local attraction was just up the line, something they'd not want to miss. The guard must have told the engineer, because when a bridge came into sight, the train slowed. The dead man was naked except for a pair of soiled pants and a single dress shoe gleaming blackly in the late-morning sun, its lace untied. Blood clotted on his face and chest. The man's head leaned toward one shoulder, as if curious at what had befallen him. A placard dangled from his neck, the word *Hun* charring the wood. Try to escape, one of the guards told them, and that will happen to you.

After a while he and Hank changed places. Though bringing up the barrel was harder work, Walter was glad to be out of the hole. But Hank's missing hand made his working below difficult and much slower, so after lunch Walter stayed in the hole until Laurel called them for dinner. They were both so mud sodden that Laurel laid clean clothes on the old well's corbelled head. He and Walter stripped and shared the soap and water.

"That was as full a day's work as we've ever done," Hank said as they dressed. "I'm sorry you're the one has to stay in that hole all the while, but with me down there it'd be Christmas before we hit water."

Hank went on inside but Walter lingered. He looked up at the cliff. With the shorter days, it seemed even more massive, further narrowing the light. So different from the ocean's endless above. He suddenly remembered the *Vaterland*'s gold sextant. Another detail for Laurel. In the last days, the ship had become more vivid to him than any time since he had left New York. Sometimes it was as if he saw it more clearly now than when he'd been on it. Laurel too. She now knew half the ship as well as he did.

Laurel stepped out on the porch.

"We're waiting for you, Walter."

He nodded and went on inside.

CHAPTER EIGHTEEN

They had been lucky. As wearisome as the digging was, Hank and Walter at least hadn't hit more rock. They were fifty feet deep according to Hank's rough measuring, close enough that on Tuesday Hank borrowed Slidell's wagon to order the pulley. Laurel went with him to buy the dress she'd wear the day she and Walter left for New York. As they came into Mars Hill, a newsboy held up a newspaper that proclaimed ARMISTICE WITH TURKEY, beneath WAR SURE TO END SOON. Good that I did come today, Laurel thought, I may have need of that dress this very week.

"I figure that new pulley to set us back a few bucks, but it'll last till we all got gray hair," Hank said.

Laurel nodded. It would, though she and Walter wouldn't be around to see that happen. A lot of wasted work, especially if Hank couldn't sell the farm. Though with Laurel gone, she believed there was a much greater chance of finding a buyer. If it did sell, she'd take none of the money. It was part of something she wanted to be shed of completely.

Hank found a free post in front of the depot and helped Laurel off the buckboard. A sound like volleys of rifle shots came from the depot's far side.

"What the hell is that?" Hank asked, and they walked onto the depot's planking to see.

Chauncey Feith stood in front of a grandstand completed but for the steps and railing. The Boys Working Reserve wielded saws and hammers as Chauncey gave orders over the din.

"Must be part of the big to-do next week for Paul Clayton," Hank said.

"I guess there's worse they could be doing," Laurel said.

Hank nodded and turned his gaze back toward town.

"So I'll go on over to Lingefelt's and order the pulley, buy a new rope and pail, couple of other things. What about you?"

"I'm just going to the dress shop."

Hank took out his watch and checked the clock tower.

"Let's meet back here in twenty minutes."

As Hank walked up the street, Laurel looked at the town spread out before her. This could be the last time she came to Mars Hill except to board a train to leave it. As her eyes passed over the storefronts, then above to the college, she wanted to feel something besides bitterness. It wasn't all of them, Laurel told herself. There was Doctor Carter and Miss Calicut and Marcie, and Professor Mayer, he'd been kind to her. Mr. Shuler had been nice when she'd traded there, and Tillman Estep, who'd stared at the ground as he handed Laurel a five-dollar bill. To help you through until your brother gets home, Estep had said. No, Laurel thought, not all of them.

She touched the dress pocket to make sure the three silver dollars were still there. It would be a new dress for a new life. As Laurel crossed the street and stepped onto the boardwalk, she thought how good it would be to live where no one knew anything about her. People weren't supposed to be friendly in cities, but how could there not be more smiles and nods than here.

Inside the cloth shop, a group of women stood by the counter, Mrs. Dobbins on the other side. This is the last time, Laurel reminded herself, and took a deep breath. When she walked in, the women quit talking. She saw only Mrs. Dobbins's face but knew its sour expression was matched by four more. Laurel went to the back of the shop and slowly thumbed through the wooden trays, finally decided which pattern she liked best. The dress's shoulder straps were thin and would reveal the birth stain, but that didn't matter to her because it didn't matter to Walter. She stepped among the bolts of cloth, wished she'd asked him his favorite color. Laurel pondered what it might be, trying to remember if he'd made special notice of her blue-checked gingham dress or yellow ribbon. If he had, she couldn't recall it. Then she remembered something else.

The women were talking again and their tone and glances toward the back of the store made the topic clear. Laurel found a striped cloth she liked but instead decided on a solid. She checked the pattern and turned toward the counter.

"I need five yards of this one," Laurel said.

The women turned as one, as if offended that she'd spoken in their presence.

"Excuse me," Mrs. Dobbins said, and came around the counter with her cutting shears.

Mrs. Dobbins rolled the cloth off the bolt, cut it with quick ragged snips as an older woman came into the shop. She wore a cloche hat and a yoke-collar dress. A diamond sparkled on her hand and pearls big as marbles hung around her neck.

"Good afternoon, Mrs. Garvey," Mrs. Dobbins said, bunching the cloth and handing it to Laurel like it was a dirty dishrag.

Mrs. Dobbins bustled over to where Mrs. Garvey stood.

"What may I help you with today, ma'am?"

"I'm having a dress made for my granddaughter. Some nice silk, if you have it."

"Yes, ma'am, we have an array of lovely crepe de chines," Mrs. Dobbins said. "Over here by the window."

Mrs. Garvey examined the silk as Laurel stepped to the counter.

"Excuse me just for a moment, Mrs. Garvey," Mrs. Dobbins said.

Mrs. Dobbins took Laurel's three silver dollars and placed them in the cash register. She laid two quarters and a dime on the counter, took out a handkerchief, and wiped her hands. The women around the counter gave smirks of approval. Old biddies, that's all they are, Laurel thought. An image from childhood came to her. A hawk had grabbed a baby chick and then lost its grip. The biddy was hurt and bleeding and the other biddies began pecking it. Because that was what biddies did, she'd learned that day. They found one of their own sick or hurt and took turns pecking it to death.

"Six yards of this one," Mrs. Garvey said.

"Yes, ma'am," Mrs. Dobbins answered, and reached for the shears, "and I must tell you, Mrs. Garvey, that is the finest cloth in the store."

"You've wiping your hands," Laurel said, "you did that because you think me a witch, Mrs. Dobbins?"

Mrs. Dobbins reddened. For a few moments she stared at Laurel, then turned to Mrs. Garvey.

"The very finest cloth, Mrs. Garvey, I can assure you of that."

"So you think me a witch or not?" Laurel asked again, loud enough that Mrs. Garvey stared at her.

"So what if I do," Mrs. Dobbins hissed, and came around the counter, brushed past Laurel.

"Then you'd better warn Mrs. Garvey that I touched that silk just a few minutes ago. I hexed it, so there's no telling what might happen to her granddaughter."

Laurel picked up her change and walked outside. Hank waited by the wagon, the rope and bucket and a salt lick stashed in the bed. Laurel crossed the street. Chauncey Feith and his boys were still working on the scaffold, saws grinding amid the hammers' sharp reports. Hank unhitched Ginny and they rode up Main Street. The sun was out but a steady wind made the air chilly. Laurel raised her coat lapels and covered her neck.

"That's some fancy cloth you bought, sister," Hank said. "What will you make with it?"

"A dress."

"Looks to be for a special occasion," Hank said, and smiled. "You and Walter ain't made plans to get hitched without telling me, have you?"

You've been spiteful enough for one day, Laurel told herself, but she couldn't hold her tongue.

"You mean the way you did me?"

Hank stared at the reins.

"I was wrong to do that, wrong about some other concernings too," Hank said. "Things are going to be different. They already are. The farm's in better shape than it's ever been. The crops proved out a good harvest and the livestock's stout. It shows a prospering has come to the cove. Even Carolyn's daddy admitted as much. Now I've got Carolyn and you've got Walter and I'm figuring things to only keep getting better, don't you?"

"Yes," Laurel said, and she did believe they would. It just wouldn't be here.

"The way people see us, it's changing."

"For you," Laurel answered.

"But it will for you too," Hank said, "just give it time. I've been thinking about what lays ahead for all of us. After a year or two Carolyn and me could move back. It's the gloaminess that bothers her, so we could build a house on the ridge near the creek. Cut down some trees and we'd have sunshine aplenty. You and Walter could do the same, leave that darksome cabin to the spiders and salamanders. The bottomland has some rich soil, Daddy was right about that, and it's been fallow so long we'll have bumper crops for sure. All of us could make a good life there, and you and me could finally have a real family, with cousins and aunts and uncles. Folks won't have the least cause to shun us."

The way Hank described it, Laurel could almost believe it might happen. It was like a map unfurled with just enough dots and names to look real. A last beguiling to keep her here, not by Hank but by the cove itself, allowing her to dream the place different. But it wouldn't be different, not really. There would always be folks like Mrs. Dobbins. Even Walter, what would he believe, and blame, if the first cow died of milk fever, or a hailstorm flailed the life out of three months' work. If she got pregnant and something went wrong.

"The dress I'm making," Laurel said, "it's a surprise for Walter, so don't let on."

"I won't," Hank said.

They were on the Marshall pike now, and Laurel turned her mind to the *Vaterland*'s B deck first, moving through the Ritz-Carlton restaurant and the wintergarden's palm trees and flowers and gilt latticework, then on through the ship's library with its glassed bookcase and blue oriental rug, finally the social hall, the biggest room of all and where the orchestra had played. There were two elevators and three winding staircases with bronze banisters, windows framed with pilasters and oak walls, four oil paintings of Pandora. There was a half-moon stage with a grand piano and above it all a glass ceiling.

As the wagon jolted onto the wayfare, Laurel moved on to the A deck, starting in the smoking room with its brass lanterns dangling from the ceiling, stained-glass windows, the white-stone fireplace Walter told her a grown man could stand in, its andirons heavy as another ship's anchor. By the time they got to Slidell's, Laurel had imagined all of the A, B, C, and D decks. It was like a jigsaw puzzle in her head, some pieces missing but enough that Laurel was starting to have it all connect.

Slidell came out and helped get Ginny unhitched and back in her stable. Stay and have a drink if you're not averse, he told Hank, so Laurel walked on alone to the cove. Walter was by the shed, chopping logs into kindling. She took the cloth and pattern to her room and came back outside.

"Be careful," Laurel said as she approached. "Those fingers of yours are going to have to keep us out of the poorhouse."

Laurel took the axe from his hand, leaned closer, and kissed him softly on the mouth.

"Let's go inside where it's warmer," Laurel said. "Hank's having a dram with Slidell, so we got some time to talk."

But Walter shook his head and led her a few yards into the

woods. They faced the notch to watch for Hank. Overcautious, Laurel thought, but not to be swayed in the matter. He'd yet to speak a single word on the porch or in the cabin.

"Hank talked to me today about him and Carolyn coming here to live with us," Laurel said. "It's not likely crossed his mind we could be leaving."

"And that is how we want it to stay," Walter said.

"I know," Laurel said.

She took his right hand, brought it around her waist, and settled her back against his chest.

"A newspaper claimed the war's all but over. It said there's been an armistice with Turkey."

"Perhaps so," Walter said. "After so long, it is an amazement anyone remains to fight."

"When it does end," Laurel said, "all I will take with me I can wrap in a bedsheet. Ten minutes and I'll be ready. I want us to leave that very day, even if we have to walk to Mars Hill."

Laurel saw Hank coming down from the notch. Still a while though, before he got to the cabin.

"We have time for you to tell me about the E deck."

"There was a swimming bath," Walter said, "and twin marble staircases led down to it, and a statue made of black marble."

"What was it a statue of?" Laurel asked.

"An angel," Walter said.

CHAPTER NINETEEN

On that Sunday afternoon four months ago, the first thing Chauncey had seen as he crossed the river was the Mountain Park Hotel looming over the whole town. It was even grander than he had supposed, four stories high with two cupolas rising even higher. He'd heard the hotel's interior was spartan since becoming part of a prison camp, but it was still a magnificent building the *Vaterland*'s officers were allowed to occupy. One of them stood on the hotel porch, and because of the white beard and white uniform, Chauncey knew which officer it was. Beside the hotel were a dozen barracks and around them wells and coal bunkers and even a blacksmith shop. A fence surrounded the hotel and barracks, but though it looked to be a good ten feet high, Chauncey noted that a man who would risk a few barbs in his hands could scale it easy enough. He slowly passed the barracks and saw the Germans milling about. Some played cards or pinochle while others smoked and lounged. They weren't wearing shackles and it had looked to Chauncey more like a church camp than a prison. One Hun was at the fence, talking to a pretty young woman outside the wire, a local girl from the look of her flour-print dress. No one appeared to care that she and the Hun could be passing information or a weapon. As he passed, Chauncey saw their fingers touched through the wire.

The camp entrance was between the hotel and the barracks, so Chauncey had parked, gathered his notebook and pen, and crossed the perimeter road. Two guards with shotguns slouched in chairs outside the open gate. Neither bothered to look up until Chauncey was right in front of them. The shorter man raised his right hand slightly, unsure if he was expected to salute.

What can we do for you, sir? the shorter man had asked and Chauncey answered that he'd wanted to see if the prison camp was as disgraceful as he'd been hearing and he'd already seen enough to confirm that it was. You don't know the half of it, the shorter guard said as a farmer passed through the gate with a basket of tomatoes. Us red-blooded Americans is so rationed out we're near starving and these Huns get plenty to eat. They even got hot water.

Chauncey nodded at the Hun and the local girl, who still had their fingers twined, and asked what the hell kind of prison camp it was that allowed such a thing. This ain't no prison camp, the taller guard had answered, saucy like, it's for internees, not soldiers nor spies. Then the guard had given pretty near a speech about how the Germans never caused a bit of trouble and that there were musicians amongst them who played concerts folks in Hot Springs came to and how when the bridge got washed out the Germans rebuilt it. The other guard piped in and said he did have to admit the Germans had done a crackerjack job on the bridge. Chauncey had finally quit listening and started writing notes for his report. When he asked the guards their names, the shorter one said what for and Chauncey answered for being two of the sorriest guards he'd ever seen in his life. Of course the tall one bowed up and said there'd been nary an escape on his watch. Chauncey had answered that the Huns were afraid if they did get out they might end up in a real prison camp instead of a health resort.

Chauncey had driven back to Mars Hill that June Sunday and gone straight to his office and typed up a full report on the camp and sent it to Captain Arnold, who sent the report on to his superior. Chauncey hadn't been asked for any further information or been called to Washington to testify or anything like that, but now it was November, and the Hot Springs Germans had been hauled down to Fort Oglethorpe in Georgia, a real prison camp where they had machine guns and a dead line on the perimeter and the prisoners weren't mollycoddled but made to work in a rock quarry all day.

Chauncey raised his eyes from the newspaper. He looked out the window and watched a farmer enter the post office. A fish wrapper, that was all the good the *Marshall Sentinel* was. From what he'd just read, the German who'd escaped in August did so to keep from going to Fort Oglethorpe, which just confirmed what Chauncey had told that smartass guard. The Hun still hadn't been recaptured and could be anywhere by now, maybe even sneaked back to Germany in a U-boat.

But that wasn't the worst of it. Above the article was a photograph of Commodore Ruser shaking a guard's hand. The old fool was still wearing his white uniform and Chauncey remembered how Ruser had stood on the hotel's front porch with a pipe in his mouth and his hands behind his back, looking out like he was still on the prow of the *Vaterland*. When the commodore and his crew first came to Madison County, the *Sentinel* had made a big to-do over them and the tub they'd been on, spouting off about the *Vaterland* being the biggest ship ever built and there were three million rivets and fifteen thousand electric lights and so on. It was nothing but Hun propaganda, complete with a picture of the *Vaterland* in New York Harbor, a German flag clear as day on the ship's masthead.

Chauncey himself had to set the record straight, doing his own interviewing by telephone. He'd found plenty the newspaper didn't bother to mention, like how the crew had sabotaged the *Vaterland*, everything from hacksawing piston rods to throwing machine parts overboard. Or that the *Vaterland*'s crew rigged steam pipes so they'd bust once enough pressure built up, the vilest sort of treachery because they hoped to sink the ship with a bunch of Americans onboard. Then, to top it all, once the United States made its declaration of war, Ruser complained it was wrong to arrest German civilians—this after his country sank the *Lusitania* and drowned a thousand American and British civilians, most of them women and children. Chauncey had written it all up and taken it to the *Sentinel*'s office and demanded they print it and they damn well had.

Chauncey laid the newspaper on his desk and went to the window and again looked across the street. Two old women gabbed on the post office steps so he sat back down. He folded the newspaper and dropped it in the trash can. Chauncey wondered if it had been his report that had gotten the Hot Springs camp closed.

No one had ever given him credit as such, but what was the surprise in that. At least the Huns were gone. The only shame was Miss Yount and that professor hadn't been hauled off with them.

The tower clock rang ten times and Chauncey got up and looked toward the post office again. What's got you so all-fired interested in the mail of a sudden? Marvin Alexander had asked three weeks ago. Before he'd thought better, Chauncey answered he was expecting a letter from Governor Bickett. When he'd entered the post office the next morning and found his mailbox empty, Marvin had winked at Georgina Singleton. Guess the governor has a few other matters to attend to before he writes his pen pal, Marvin had said, and Georgina Singleton thought it quite the josh. After that, Chauncey thought about sending one of the boys to check his box and not give the postmaster the satisfaction of seeing him disappointed, but that meant waiting until late afternoon. Each morning Chauncey would look out his window, knowing the governor's letter could be just across the street, not even a stone's throw away, waiting for him. After an hour or two he'd not be able to stand it and would go check, but only when Marvin Alexander and his big mouth were in the post office alone.

Chauncey did the same this morning, waiting awhile then crossing the street, expecting yet another smartass smile or quip. But today Marvin Alexander told Chauncey his letter had come and handed it to him. At first Chauncey thought it might be a jape on the postmaster's part, but then he saw the gold seal and typed return address. His own name was typed too, *Sergeant Chauncey Feith*, followed by *Mars Hill North Carolina*.

"You going to open it?" Alexander asked.

Where are your smartass words and smile now, Chauncey almost answered but instead placed the letter in his uniform's shirt pocket, like it was nothing more than a ticket stub, and walked out. In the office, he sat at his desk and laid the letter before him. He read the addresses again, then turned the letter over and let his index finger rub the gold imprint of the statehouse seal. He opened his drawer and took out a brass letter opener, decided it was too blunt so took out his penknife instead. He placed the blade tip on the fold's edge and slowly let the steel slit the letter's top. Outside, a gangly youth read a recruitment poster on the window, but Chauncey ignored him and carefully unfolded the letter.

Dear Sergeant Feith,

It is with great regret that I will be unable to attend your homecoming parade honoring one of our heroic soldiers, but the exigencies of office will not allow my participation. Nevertheless, I wish to inform you and the citizens of Mars Hill and Madison County that there will be an official proclamation recognizing the celebration, and it will be read in the statehouse chambers. Thank you for your gracious invitation and your hard work on behalf of our brave soldiers. Americans such as yourself are, too often, the unsung heroes of our country's fight against the Central Powers. Therefore, the proclamation will honor you by name as well as Paul Clayton.

Sincerely,
Governor Thomas Walter Bickett

Chauncey knew he should be disappointed by the governor's response, but as he reread the letter it was hard to be. At the homecoming they could have the proclamation read aloud by Senator Zeller, though perhaps not the part about Chauncey himself. After all, the event was to honor Paul. Yes, he decided, he'd have the part about himself left out, insist it be left out. Still, he would have the letter framed, and he was going to hang it on the wall directly behind where he now sat, or better, on the wall next to the window. It would give people like Marvin Alexander and anybody else pause before they disrespected him again. Though what they thought didn't matter. Why care what a bunch of mountain grills thought when the governor of North Carolina had called Sergeant Chauncey Feith a hero.

CHAPTER TWENTY

"I figure us to hit the real water today," Hank said as they stepped off the porch. "We'll be ever glad of that, won't we?"

Walter nodded. The last three weeks had been the hardest work in his life. They had labored from early morning to dusk each day and almost all that time he was in the hole's darkness. Pointless work too, though Walter wasn't as convinced of that as he had once been. Hank spoke of a future in the cove so idyllic, for all of them, that Laurel might waver. After all the work the three of them had done, even he felt some attachment to the farm.

Walter was about to get in the barrel when he saw Slidell tethering his horse to the porch rail. The older man set two burlap sacks on the steps.

"Brought some apples besides the horsehair for your batter," Slidell said as he joined them. "I reckon you about done since you need it."

"We got some seep two days ago so we'll soon be there," Hank said, "but it's been some onerous work, especially for Walter. He's the one wallering down in the dark. Thank the Lord that place on Balsam has a good well. I'd rather fight a hellcat than do another."

"Come hard weather it'll be a blessing though," Slidell said.

"I told Walter the same."

Slidell let his gaze sweep over the pasture.

"It's a wonder how much you two have got done since August. You've turned this place into a real farm. It's good to see such a thing after all these years. Anyway, I wanted to tell you I'm going to those big doings for Paul Clayton tomorrow, so if you want to ride with me you're welcome."

"I may take you up on that," Hank said. "I ordered my pulley from Neil Lingefelt and it might be in."

"Just be at my place midmorning," Slidell said. "If you don't go and it's in, I'll fetch your pulley back."

"If I go, you mind if Laurel tags along, maybe even this fellow here?" Hank asked, and turned to Walter. "I'm thinking it cause enough to finally get you to town."

"That's going to be a crowd of folks," Slidell said. "He might rather go when there's not such a ruckus."

Walter nodded.

"Okay," Hank said, "but you need to leave this cove sometime. People can't get to know you if you don't."

"I need to get on back," Slidell said. "Looks to be Indian summer's set in, so it's a good day to cut firewood, maybe clean out my spring."

"If you've not had breakfast, Laurel can fix you some eggs, gravy you some cornbread too."

"I ate but I'll go in and say howdy," Slidell said, and went on to the cabin.

"I guess we better get at it," Hank said. "Standing in that water will be the worst part, but you only got to dig waist deep and we'll be done but for the walling. Warm as it is, at least you won't sprout icicles when you come back up."

Walter climbed into the barrel and settled his feet on the bottom. He grasped the rope and, as he did every time, studied its twines for fraying. He looked at the ridge above the creek. The trees had shed most of their leaves and the lack of greenery made the mountains starker, more firmly locked to the land. The oldest mountains in the whole world, one of the guards had claimed, and today they looked it, stark and gray-brown as a daguerreotype. As the winch creaked and groaned, Walter watched the farm sink into the ridge and the ridge sink into the wedge of sky and then before him was only the well wall darkening more with each turn of the winch.

When the barrel finally hit bottom, the hole above was no bigger than a button. The air was moldy at this depth, like behind a long shut cellar door. Walter pulled himself out of the barrel and began digging. The dirt gave easily with each stab of the shovel. He thrust the curved point deeper and it broke through the last damp soil into mud. His boots were soon submerged and he had to crouch instead of kneel. The shovel's lift no longer rasped but made a sucking sound followed by the soil's soggy clap as it fell into the barrel.

It was disconcerting to feel but not see water rising over his ankles and then calves. The water was not the teeth-chilling cold of a brook but it was cold enough. Walter made good time for a while, but by late morning water reached his knees. He immersed his arms deeper with each gouge, trying to balance the mud on the curved steel as he lifted it to the barrel. Water sloshed on him each time he raised the shovel.

When he hauled Walter up for lunch, Hank judged the depth by the waterline on Walter's waist and declared the well deep enough. Hank asked if he wanted to change into dry clothes but Walter shook his head.

"Yeah," Hank said, "I guess it don't much matter since they'll be soppy soon as you're back in there."

Laurel brought their lunch and the three of them sat on the grass. The wet clothes clung to him, and though the food was warm, several times he shivered. Hank noticed and offered to go into the well, but Walter shook his head, as he did when Laurel said she'd get him a dry shirt.

"Slidell told me Paul Clayton's homecoming is tomorrow," Laurel said as they finished.

"You of a mind to go?" Hank asked. "It's a good time for a holiday with this well all but done."

"No, but I was thinking that if you were Walter and me might have us a picnic."

Hank shook his head.

"I pondered it, but the thought of Chauncey Feith speechifying in front of Paul has soured me on it. I'll go see Paul once the hubbub is over. He'll need a visit more then than tomorrow. But you all go ahead and do your picnic while you have a nice day. Soon as this warm spell ends the hard weather's coming."

Laurel started to gather the dishes.

"You mind helping a few minutes before you go back in?" Hank asked. "I'd feel better with your hands on that far winch."

They filled the barrel and Hank placed his hand on the lip,

pushed so the barrel swayed back and forth a few moments, a scraping within as one rock shifted against another.

"You don't need but a foot or so above the waterline, Walter," Hank said. "Just start at the bottom and press them in the mud good slantways. After that, the water will hold them in place."

Walter nodded.

"Keep a high grip too, what with the weight of the rocks in it," Hank added. "That way even if something gives way you'll dangle until I get you back up."

Laurel set herself in front of the far winch, hands already on the handle. Walter reached for the rope with his right hand.

"This is the last time you'll be in that hole," Hank said. "Get this done and all that's left is corbelling the well guard and building a scaffold. That's a trifle after all this."

Walter set his right foot onto the iron lip. The barrel dipped and for a moment his left foot touched only air. A rock tumbled out and he did not hear it hit the well floor. Then both feet were on the lip, his hands holding so tight that Walter felt the twists of the hemp, even individual strands, as the barrel swayed back and forth, finally stilled. Only then did he move his feet inside the barrel, rocks shifting to accommodate his weight.

"You're sure it's safe, Hank?" Laurel asked.

"Safe as it can be," Hank answered, "especially if you keep your hands on the winch. Ready, Walter?"

He nodded and Hank cranked the winch counterclockwise. Walter heard the extra weight in the rub of the twine, the louder creak of the windlass. He tightened his grip to take as much weight off his feet as possible, because what frightened him most was the barrel's bottom giving way like a trapdoor. Walter closed his eyes, though even open there wasn't light enough to see. He tried to breathe slower, calmer. A rock shifted and he caught his breath.

Finally, the barrel touched water. The rope slackened and Walter gave two quick jerks. He let go of the rope and lowered himself into the seep as the bucket drifted upward to give him room to work. The water felt colder than when he had quit earlier. Deeper too. Not a lot deeper, just a few inches, but enough to notice. He took a stone from the barrel, shifted it to his right hand, and immersed his arm and shoulder while looking upward to keep his face dry. He pressed the rock firmly against the wall. He took another and did the same and after the eleventh he had the first layer. The cold water had not bothered him while shoveling but now chill bumps covered his arms. He began the second tier, not having to immerse himself quite as deep, though that did not lessen the cold.

Walter was halfway through the last tier when the rocks ran out. He swung the barrel back and forth and it rose. As he waited for Hank to refill the barrel, he could not stop shivering. The water felt colder by the second and he wondered what that meant. Finally, the barrel began descending. Walter whispered for it to hurry, but it seemed to be moving through amber. He touched his waist and it appeared the water was higher than just minutes before. He remembered what the guard had said about caves and underwater rivers with trout pale and blind from the lack of light. The guard had said one moment you were on solid footing and then you were in water so dark and deep you would never find your way back to the surface.

Finishing the last tier should have been the easiest part, but his hands shook so much the rocks were slippery as fish. Walter dropped a rock and did not try to find it, just reached for another. He finally finished the last tier and swung the barrel to signal Hank. Five minutes and you will be out, Walter told himself, but as he was getting in the barrel he lost his grip, fell backward and was immersed head to toe. He came up sputtering water as the barrel rocked back and forth and began ascending. Walter grabbed the rim to pull himself in but his hands slipped free and the barrel rose out of his grasp. No face above parsed the button of light.

He shivered harder and each breath brought less air. The earth beneath him felt thinner, mere inches between him and a river that would sweep him into some fathomless pool where no light survived. He did not move because one foot lifted and set back down might plunge the rest of him into water. It's only in your mind, Walter told himself, but now he could not help believing that the earthen floor was about to give way. A deep suck of air opened a space in his upper chest. His chin lifted and he readied a shout. He clamped his chattering teeth at the last moment and what issued forth was a low muffled groan. He took deep quick breaths through his nose and kept his lips pressed tight.

The barrel stopped.

"I'm sending it back," Hank shouted.

The barrel descended, still moving through amber, but moving. You would hear the water if it were so close, Walter reassured himself. But not if water filled the cavern to the ceiling. There would be no sound now and none when he was immersed. He would be in an inescapable darkness but, even worse, a place of endless silence. Forever. Walter reached out and pressed his splayed hand into the wall's moist dirt. He held it there and watched the barrel sink toward him.

Finally, the barrel was within reach and he grabbed the rope with one hand and the rim with the other. Walter half-pulled and half-toppled his body onto the lip, held the rope with both hands and placed hand over fist until he was completely in. The barrel rose. The hole appeared impossibly far away, and small, so small it could never widen enough to allow him through. The rope creaked and the barrel swayed with each crank, the hole still no larger than a silver dollar. Walter shifted his grip as he imagined threads of hemp unraveling with each turn of the winch. He closed his eyes and pressed his forehead against his clenched hands as if to buttress them. The air became less dank, and then he could feel light settling on his eyelids. He opened his eyes and looked up and the well mouth had rounded to the size of a cymbal. The muscles in his hands and forearms burned, but he was afraid to loosen them for a single moment.

His head broke through and the earth bobbled and then leveled around him. Hank pulled the barrel away from the well and Walter spilled out. He steadied himself on his knees, leaning so one palm lay flat against the ground. Laurel came out of the cabin, running toward him arms outstretched, already reaching to hold him. She fell before him, her hands on his shoulders.

Hank kneeled beside him too.

"You okay?" Hank asked.

Walter nodded and started to rise but Hank's hand pressed firm against his shoulder.

"Rest a minute. I'm a damn fool for not spelling you. I should of known better than to leave you down there that long."

Walter tried to rise again and Hank shifted his grip to Walter's bicep. Laurel took the other arm and he stood.

"I'll go back down," Hank said.

Walter waved his hand dismissively at the remaining rocks.

"You mean it's done?"

He nodded.

"Okay then," Hank said. "I'll go to the barn and batter us up some chinking, but you need to get out of them soggy clothes and warm up."

"Come on," Laurel said, and took Walter's hand.

They walked around the cabin to the old well. Laurel drew a bucket of water and brought fresh clothes, a towel and washcloth. He stripped and washed, put on the new clothes. Laurel had started a fire so he sat by the hearth. She leaned over the back of his chair until her face pressed against his.

"Tell me you're okay, with words. Please, I need to hear you say it."

"I'm fine," Walter said, his voice low though the door was shut.

Laurel kissed him, let her cheek resettle against his. The fire began to warm him. He shivered less and then not at all. He raised his hand and let his fingertips slowly trace the fall of Laurel's hair from ear to shoulder. There was a joyousness in just the touching, the lithe way the strands separated and regathered, and the wonder was that he had not noticed before. So much more to know, he thought. So much.

"I've a surprise for you," Laurel said, "what I've been working on in my room. I was going to save it for the day we left, but I don't want to wait. Since it's not muddy, I'll wear it tomorrow for our picnic."

Laurel put another log on the fire, a covey of orange sparks ascending as the wood resettled on the andirons. She pulled a chair beside him.

"I want to take you through the ship," Laurel said. "I think I can see every part of it now. We've got time. Hank will have to clean up before he comes in."

Laurel started with the *reichskriegflagges* on the two mastheads and worked her way through the top deck and the A B

C and D decks and last the four propellers. She asked if she'd forgotten anything, and he shook his head.

"I can believe in it now," Laurel said. "It's as real to me as it is to you, but there is one more thing."

"What is that?" Walter asked.

"You and me," Laurel answered. "But I can see that too. We're on the top deck and all around us is blue water and blue sky."

Walter smiled.

"Can you see it?" Laurel asked.

"Yes," he answered, and he could.

That night as Walter drifted toward sleep, the sensation of being in the well's depths startled him awake, his heart pounding as he lay in the dark. Think about coming out of there, he told himself, think about Laurel and how the first thing you saw was her running toward you, light all around and her arms already reaching out to hold you.

V

CHAPTER TWENTY-ONE

When you're sparking, it's all dandelions and honey, Marcie had told her, but once you're around someone every day, things you didn't much notice before, like the way he slurps his soup or don't doff his muddy boots, or even the littlest thing like a tune he keeps whistling or how he lays kindling, nags at you like a sore tooth. Of course you're showing your failings too, and he's noticing them, and there'll be days when you'll fuss and both have the sulks afterward. But I'm glad I done it, Marcie said. Oh, there's evenings you're both too frazzled to say more than a few words to each other and times he'll be in the field all day and you in the house and you'll not sight him for hours at a time, but you know he's close by. Maybe calling it being hitched ain't the prettiest way to say you're married, but it's the truth to my mind and true in a good way, because you're working together and depending on each other, and you're sharing the load. There's a blissfulness to that sharing, like when your little chap does something for the first time, holds his spoon or makes a cute sound, and it'd be nothing to anyone else but a marveling to you and him, because it's all part of something that couldn't be in the world but that the two of you brung it in together.

Yes, Laurel thought as she took the bread for their picnic from the stove, it'll not always be dandelions and honey, but that's okay. The cooking fire had warmed the cabin so much that she opened the door. Hank was using the hammer to loosen the rocks from the old well's chinking while Walter carried them across the yard and set them beside the new well. There were still moments, mornings walking to the henhouse or cooking, afternoons the cliff wedged out the day's last light, when her mind would fix on the worst imaginings—that once Walter was back outside the cove and around other women he'd realize he didn't have to settle for her, or, no matter what Walter told her otherwise, he was just wanting a safe place to wait out the war, that the very day an armistice happened he'd pack up and leave, alone. But only moments, because then their eyes would meet or hands touch, or just the memory of such a moment, and she could believe again.

Laurel placed the bread in a tin and stepped out on the porch. Hank and Walter were raising the rock circle that would make the new well head. Walter selected a rock and tried to fit it in one spot and when that didn't work he tried another. All the while Hank used a trowel to chink the gaps with manure and the horsehair from Slidell's barn. There were beans to thread and hang and a picnic basket to fix, but Laurel decided that could wait a little while.

"Come to help now that all the hard work's done," Hank teased, but he and Walter looked pleased to have her with them.

Laurel began filling the gaps too, sometimes trying half a dozen rocks before one locked into place. There was a pleasure in it, like solving a puzzle. The wall rose steadily around the hole and by midmorning it was done.

"Me and Walter can get the scaffolding finished by noon," Hank said, "then you all can go on your picnic."

As they walked into the front yard, Laurel saw not even a single layer of rock rimmed the old well.

"A varmint could fall in there," Laurel said, "so we best get our drinking water from the springhouse."

While the men walked to the shed to get the hammer and nails and planks, Laurel fetched a sack of beans from the alcove and went into the cabin. She began threading the pole beans and knotting the string ends to the rafters while the men hammered the wood to build the scaffolding. By the time these beans are parched, we may be in New York and shed of this place and its ever-always miserableness, Laurel thought. And yet, she knew, if the cove had not been bleak and lonely, Walter wouldn't have stopped here to hide or her family come here to live. Would she wish it all away—her family coming to this cove and all the bad things that had happened because of their coming, the shunning and aloneness, what Jubel and others had done to her—wish her family had instead stayed in Tennessee where a birthmark was just a birthmark and the sky held on to the sun all day?

The hammering stopped and Laurel heard the men out by the old well washing up. You go on in, I'll put the tools up, Hank said. Walter came up the steps and Laurel turned toward the door. He stepped inside, smiling as he walked across the room, his arms opening to embrace her. No, Laurel thought, I'd live every miserable day of it again, just for this moment.

CHAPTER TWENTY-TWO

Chauncey had stayed up late to confirm the train's departure from Washington. Even when he did get in bed, the coming day's responsibilities were like cockleburs prickling away sleep. He told his mother to bring breakfast to his room and then his lunch while he fussed over his speech, making changes first with a pencil before writing a final copy in ink. When the ink dried, he read the speech a last time before taking the fresh-pressed uniform from his closet. He put on the khaki shirt and breeches, then the socks and the garrison shoes, retying the laces twice before the bows were the exact same size. Chauncey strapped on the leggings and his Pershing Liberty belt that holstered the Colt pistol. He aligned the buckle with the breeches' top button, then took the tunic off its hanger and put it on, last the campaign hat. As he settled himself in front of the dressing mirror, Chauncey knew that he had done all he could. He'd worked out all the music and marching wheres and whens with the grammar school and high school and he'd talked Benjamin Parton into donating nails and wood for the grandstand and he'd supervised every drag of a saw and every swing of a hammer. He'd gotten the *Marshall Sentinel* to write a front-page article about the homecoming and figured out exactly who'd do what during the actual ceremony. Chauncey had even purchased the boys new brown leather shoes and paid for them with his own money.

He turned his gaze to the window. The sun was out. After months of planning, the day of the homecoming had finally come, and now the weather, which had been the one worry outside his control, had aligned itself as well. Chauncey looked at the man enclosed within the mirror's quartersawn frame and made a final appraisal, moving up from the gleaming tap toes of the garrison boots to the knife-sharp creases in the breeches to the tunic and its polished blackened bronze buttons and the collar with the RS and US aligned and the campaign hat's centered blue cord. There wasn't the slightest flaw. He raised his right arm and gave a crisp snap of the wrist, practicing the salute he'd give when Paul came off the train. Sergeant Chauncey Feith would square his shoulders and, even though he was a higher rank, salute the private first and hold that salute until Paul was seated and the band began to play. He looked in the mirror one more time and picked up his speech and the copy he'd made of Governor Bickett's letter and went downstairs. His mother gave him a kiss and told him how handsome he looked and his father shook his hand and told Chauncey how proud he was.

Outside, he scanned the sky. Gray clouds bunched on the horizon but they'd not arrive until after the ceremony. No breeze swayed the weathervane so he could place Governor Bickett's proclamation on the podium, which was much more dignified and respectful than holding it up like a dinner menu. After that it wouldn't matter if the other five pages sailed clear to Raleigh, because Chauncey didn't need a written speech to tell about the day Paul Clayton asked to be part of the Boys Working Reserve and Chauncey had known right away this young man was destined to be a hero by the way he comported himself, no slouching or rocking back on his heels but standing tall from the start. After just three weeks Paul had become the troop's leader and it wasn't just that he was the oldest at seventeen but because Paul Clayton led by example and never shirked his duty. The day Paul turned eighteen, he was at the recruiting office with his mother to sign the papers. If Tillman Estep had the nerve to show up at the ceremony, Chauncey would pause and look Estep right in the eye and say Paul Clayton wasn't the kind of soldier who waited to be conscripted. He would recite from memory every medal and ribbon Paul had received and say that Tennesseans could toot their horn about Alvin York all they wanted but North Carolina had a soldier every bit the equal of Alvin York and that soldier's name was Paul Clayton. Then Chauncey would step back and salute Paul again and Senator Zeller would have his say and the band would start playing and keep playing and the band and the schoolchildren would march down Main Street and following them would be Jack leading the troop and they'd march all the way back to the high school. That Hun-loving professor up on the hill wouldn't have to fiddle with his gimcrack harness to hear it and Miss Yount would damn well hear it too and she'd not be able to raise a gnarled finger to her lips to hush it.

Nevertheless, as he came closer to town and heard a radio playing, Chauncey admitted to himself there had been one thing besides bad weather that he'd hoped wouldn't happen, though thinking about it even now made him feel a little guilty. He knew he was being hard on himself. It was only human to want something you'd worked so hard for so long to be a success, but it still twinged his conscience that for weeks whenever an automobile horn honked or a church bell rang his first thought had been *please don't let it be over*. But November ninth had come and the war was not over but that wasn't Chauncey Feith's fault because whatever he'd wished or not wished about the war ending didn't matter. It was just something he'd thought, nothing more, and a thought couldn't change what happened an ocean away.

Chauncey walked briskly up Patterson Street. At the corner of Patterson and Main he stopped and set his right toe behind his left heel and made an about face. He stepped onto the boardwalk planking and passed Parton's Outdoor Goods, Linkletter's Café, and Shuler's Apothecary. All three had shades drawn and CLOSED signs on the doors. Across the street Ben Lusk ushered a customer out of the barbershop. He'd taken off his white smock and had a key in his hand. Feith Savings and Loan was shuttered and even the Turkey Trot had shut its doors, a couple of forlorn drunks lingering by the entrance. Chauncey stepped off the sidewalk and followed the train tracks to the depot.

A crowd was already gathering, some adorned in silk dresses and spiffy suits while others milled about in overalls and smocks sewn from flour sacks. There were hunched old men with canes, shouting schoolchildren, matronly women with parasols, young mothers with babies, and some professors and students. As

Chauncey made his way to the grandstand, all who saw him nodded or smiled or tipped their hats. Children ran up and saluted him and several people patted his shoulder and held out their hands to shake his. Jubel Parton said Chauncey couldn't have picked a prettier day for a parade and Georgina Singleton agreed and told him the whole town appreciated all the hard work he'd done. Professor Dukes, who'd signed the petition and quoted Chauncey at a faculty meeting on the limits of free speech, spoke of how proud he was of Chauncey and Marvin Alexander said the same.

Chauncey nodded to all who gave him kind looks and kind words but he didn't speak or smile. It wasn't that Chauncey Feith didn't appreciate the praise but a modest demeanor reflected the truth, that he was merely a soldier doing his duty. To respond any other way would be a bad example for the boys. As soon as Jack saw Chauncey, he lined the others up beside the grandstand and they all saluted. The boys looked impressive in their new shoes and washed and ironed shirts and pants. Chauncey returned the salute and blinked back a tear, because what he felt was gratitude that he'd had the opportunity to mold such fine boys into men. He told Jack that the boys wouldn't need to line up until one forty-five and could be at ease until then. Since the library visit, there'd been times Jack had forgotten his sirs and salutes, but today Jack said yes sir loud and clear and gave a proper salute before the boys broke formation and mingled with the ever-growing crowd.

Chauncey checked the clock tower and saw that the metal minute hand would soon begin its climb upward to one fifty-five. When he looked over at the depot, he saw that Boyce Clayton was on the porch with his sister-in-law Belle, a woman who had raised a hero though she'd had to do it alone after losing her husband in a logging accident. She sat on the bench and people took her hand and spoke. Mrs. Clayton raised a balled-up handkerchief and dabbed her eyes. Chauncey was glad once again that he'd decided to place her on the stage and have Jack escort her to a seat beside Chauncey and Senator Zeller.

The crowd had gathered around the grandstand and depot while others lined both sides of the railroad tracks. Chauncey glanced down Main Street, looking for the automobile bringing Congressman Zeller but instead saw Tillman Estep walking toward him. A mother picked up her child as Estep approached, turned so the child wouldn't see Estep's face. Showing up to bask in a real hero's fame, Chauncey thought as he watched Estep make his way through the crowd, and quite willing to frighten children with his Halloween mask of a face to do it.

Chauncey heard his name shouted. Jack stood on the depot platform, waving frantically for him to come. He walked rapidly toward the depot where Boyce Clayton gestured at a paper in his hand. At first Chauncey thought it was a telegram saying the train had been delayed. Then his stomach knotted as he realized the telegram might contain news that would ruin everything he'd worked so hard on. But as Chauncey stepped onto the platform, he saw it wasn't a telegram but a wanted poster.

"Me and Ansel, we've seen this fellow," Boyce said.

Chauncey shoved closer.

"Where?"

"At Hank Shelton's place. This fellow's living with them. Slidell Hampton took us down there to play music one evening and we seen him."

Linville Wray took the poster and stared at the etching.

"Let's go get the damn Hun."

"Count me in," Jubel Parton said. "Somebody get my horse and I'll fetch rifles and ammunition, and plenty of rope."

"Me and Ansel are with you," Boyce Clayton said.

"I can go on ahead and get my dogs," Linville Wray said, "just in case he tries to hightail it."

But what about the ceremony, Chauncey almost said, as men prepared to get their horses.

"How come you just to notice it was him today?" Chauncey asked.

"There wasn't much chance little as we get to town," Boyce said.

"That's right," Ansel added. "Slidell and Hank both said he was from New York. How was we to know the otherwise?"

"The when don't matter," Jubel said. "We know now and we're wasting time."

"You going to lead them, Sergeant Feith?" Wilber asked, standing beside Chauncey now.

"Of course he is," Jack said, "and we'll be with him."

"I'm thinking we should contact Sheriff Crockett in Marshall," Chauncey said. "I mean, a matter like this is more his jurisdiction than mine."

"Wait a damn minute," Jubel seethed. "Hell, that Hun could be in the next county by the time the sheriff gets here."

"It's called proper protocol," Chauncey stammered.

Jubel stared at him.

"I got another name to call it, Feith," Linville Wray said.

Everyone stared at him now, and on their faces, even Jack's, was the same look Chauncey had seen on the playground when he was a boy and wouldn't roughhouse and the same look he'd gotten from people like Tillman Estep and Hank Shelton and now a fourteen-year-old. All of them wanting to think the worst of Chauncey Feith. But this time would be different, he decided. He'd show them once and for all.

"Meet in front of the Turkey Trot," Chauncey said, and pushed through the crowd to get to the stable.

The men gathered on their mounts and Jubel came from the hardware store with an armful of rifles and a box of bullets, three ropes coiled around his shoulder.

"Slidell's around here somewhere," Boyce said. "I seen his wagon. Maybe he can help."

"How do we know he ain't helping that damn Hun?" Jubel asked. "You said he knew him. Besides, we ain't got time to wait."

"Let's go," Chauncey said.

He jerked the reins and turned Traveler. The horse galloped down Main Street scattering pedestrians and halting a Pierce-Arrow limousine, the astonished face of Senator Zeller behind the passenger glass. Chauncey passed the last storefront and soon caught up with Linville Wray and his wagonload of dogs. Chauncey slowed and told Linville to meet him not at the cove mouth but at Hank Shelton's place, then slapped Traveler's flank and the horse was again at full gallop. Chauncey glanced back and saw that the boys and men followed. He remembered how Boyce hardly acknowledged him three months earlier at the Turkey Trot, but by God Boyce and Ansel both were following him now and so were Jubel Parton and Linville Wray. He felt the horse beneath him, solid and assured. Traveler obeyed each tug of the reins without hesitation. Jubel and his horse briefly pulled alongside, but when they turned onto the narrower wayfare Jubel fell back and Chauncey led alone.

"Make sure your guns are loaded," Chauncey said when they got to Slidell Hampton's house.

Chauncey took a magazine from his ammo pouch, turned

so the others couldn't see his hands trembled. He pushed the magazine into the Colt's handle and pulled the slide back, released it to put a round in the chamber.

"How many guns does Hank have?" Chauncey asked Boyce.

"No more than a shotgun by my reckoning," Boyce said. "But I can't figure him to be on a German's side in a fight."

"Hank and Laurel, I don't think they know who he is," Ansel added.

"We're arresting them all," Chauncey ordered. "What's the truth and what ain't we can sort out later."

CHAPTER TWENTY-THREE

As they walked through the woods, no breeze stirred what last leaves clung to the branches, but it wasn't like the stillness before an afternoon thunderstorm or after a thick snow. Instead, it seemed the earth had paused, unsure if it wanted to turn back toward summer or move on into winter.

"When we get to New York, will we live beside the ocean?" Laurel asked.

"If not, we'll be near."

"Good," Laurel said. "I want to look at something I can't see the end of. That's how it is, isn't it, endless?"

"Yes," Walter said.

They came to the brook and made their way upstream. Laurel set the muscadine wine in the pool and they stepped onto the outcrop and unpacked the basket. The rock was warmer than last time, brighter as well since there was no haze or clouds, just a wide rising into a depthless blue. As Walter unfurled the checkered quilt, he imagined it seen from an aeroplane or zeppelin, the cloth like a flag making some human claim on this wild place.

"I should have had you bring your flute," Laurel said as she took the bread and preserves from the basket, set out the plates and napkins and knife. "But I'm of a mind we've got enough prettiness without it."

More than enough, Walter thought, with the blue sky and the stream's sparkling mica amid the flow and shoal of yellow leaves. The dress Laurel wore was pretty too, the finer cloth clinging to her body's curves, the dress's cut revealing more of her breasts and shoulders. When Laurel had first come out of her room, he had found the green color unsettling, but now he saw it for what it really was, not an omen but a confirmation that what he'd once lost had finally returned. They ate, then drank the wine. Afterward they lay down, Laurel with her head on his shoulder. Walter listened to water slide off the ledge and splash below. He closed his eyes and felt the sun take away the deep-earth dampness that had seeped into him. With the sound of the water and the way the outcrop seemed to float above the cove, it was as if they were adrift. He remembered a song he had heard in Central Park about rowing a boat because life was but a dream.

Laurel settled her hand over his. They did not talk and after a while he thought she might be asleep, but then she spoke.

"When you think about the *Vaterland*, do you ever have moments when you think it didn't exist?"

"Not recently," he said. "You have made certain of that."

"I guess so," Laurel said, and smiled. "There's so much more I want to know, know good enough not to forget. The place you were born is called Narsdorf and is in Saxony and the conservatory is in Leipzig."

Walter nodded.

"May fourth is your birthday and your sisters' names are Gertrude and Lena, and your father's name is Claus and your mother's Anna."

"Very good," he said.

For a few moments they were silent. The wine and sun had made him sleepy and he closed his eyes.

"As lonely a life as I've had in this place I'd not wish it otherwise," Laurel said, "because had it been different I wouldn't have met you. Your life, it's not been a bed of roses either."

"Easier than yours," Walter said.

"But it was hard for you at the conservatory."

"Not so bad after the first few weeks."

"And you were twelve when you went there?" Laurel asked.

"Yes, twelve."

"But now things are better," Laurel said, "so there's no need for us fret about what once was."

Laurel leaned and kissed him on the mouth. The kiss lengthened and they shed clothes and brought their bodies together, but in a drowsy way, then fell asleep with their clothes a pillow, the quilt half under and half around them. After a while they woke and dressed. For a few minutes they sat on the quilt, listening to water veil the forest's other sounds.

"I guess we better get back so I can start supper," Laurel said.

Walter helped Laurel to her feet. She brushed off the dress.

"I'll have to wash it again before we leave for New York, but it was nice wearing it for you. It made today more special."

"Yes," Walter said. "It did."

Laurel put the cups and knife and preserves in the basket, but instead of packing the quilt and wine bottle, she found four flat creek stones and placed one on each corner of the quilt. She set the wine bottle in the middle and secured it with a small cairn of rocks.

"Why are you doing so?" he asked.

"Because this might be the last time we get to picnic here. Even if it's not us or Hank and his family, somebody else will come to this cove, maybe to live. I want them to see that something happy could happen here."

Walter picked up the basket and followed Laurel off the outcrop and past the pool where she'd chilled the wine. They followed the brook's leaps and pauses into the cove.

"Maybe I'll make a pie for tonight," Laurel said. "Would you like that?"

"I would," he said.

"Slidell gave us those apples. You want that or blackberry?"

"Blackberry."

"All right," Laurel said. "But there's one condition."

"Which is?"

Laurel turned and smiled.

"You let Hank fetch the cinnamon this time."

The brook grew quieter as the land leveled. The path veered away from the water and into the woods. They were halfway to the cabin when they heard dogs barking and then a shout.

"Something's wrong," Laurel said.

Walter set the basket down and they hurried through the trees until they could see the cabin.

Hank was roped to a porch rail and a man in a uniform pointed a pistol at him. Another man tied a noose to the well's scaffolding. Boyce Clayton was in the yard with a red-headed man who held a leash in each hand, on the other ends two dogs, their long ears dragging the ground as they circled and sniffed.

"They know you're here," Laurel whispered as Ansel Clayton came from the cabin with a shirt. "Come on. Hurry."

When they got to the brook, Laurel told him to take off his shirt. He did and handed it to her.

"Wade up the creek and don't let your feet touch the bank," Laurel said. "Go to the waterfall. If I don't show up by dusk, go to your old camp. I'll come for you when it's safe."

CHAPTER TWENTY-FOUR

They made their way to where the land began its descent. The path became rockier and they passed beneath a drift of tin and bottles, on the ground salt and chips of colored glass. Chauncey knew why they'd been placed here and thought of last January when he'd asked Slidell Hampton to take the telegram about Hank's wound to Laurel. *I'd not have thought a military man to be spooked by old wives' tales*, Slidell had taunted.

The cliff's shadow engulfed them and the men as well as the boys got quieter. The air became cool and moist. By the time the ground leveled, the cliff cleaved half the sky. Chauncey had heard there were places in this cove that light had never touched, and if a man lingered long in one he'd never be able to look at the sun again. He thumbed back the Colt's safety.

Chauncey slowed and let the others ride alongside as they came out of the woods. Hank was on the porch but there was no gun visible. Even if he has one, with one hand he won't be able to aim it good, Chauncey reassured himself.

"Where's that Hun spy you're hiding?" Chauncey ordered as they dismounted.

"What are you talking about?" Hank asked.

"Walter," Boyce said, "the one what plays the fife."

"Use one of them ropes to tie him up," Chauncey ordered Jubel. "You boys help."

"He's a musician," Hank said, "from New York."

Chauncey unholstered the pistol and aimed it at Hank, willing his hand not to tremble.

"Where's your sister, helping him hide?"

"He ain't no spy," Hank said. "He can't even talk."

"Grab him," Jubel shouted, and he and the boys pinned Hank against the side railing.

The boys held Hank while Jubel bound him, leaving just enough rope to knot the ends tight around a slat.

"Where are they?" Chauncey demanded.

"You go to hell, Feith," Hank said.

Chauncey heard the hounds coming down the trail into the cove.

"We need something he's worn and them dogs will find him quick enough," Boyce said.

"Go get something you figure his," Chauncey told Ansel, "and make sure that Hun ain't hiding under a bed. Boyce, check the woodshed. Jack, take Wilber and search the barn and don't forget the loft."

"Yes, sir," Jack said.

In the side yard a scaffold had been built over the well but there was no pulley or bucket.

"You better check that well, Jubel," Chauncey said.

Jubel took a rope with him. He struck a match and peered into the well mouth, then threw the rope over the top beam and tied a noose.

"One less thing to do when we find him," Jubel said. "Once he quits kicking all we'll have to do is cut the rope."

Ansel came out of the cabin with a chambray shirt.

"You sure it's his?" Chauncey asked.

"Too small to be Hank's," Boyce said.

"When I get these damn ropes off me, I'm coming for all you sons of bitches," Hank shouted.

"Maybe we won't give you the chance, Shelton," Jubel said. "The good thing about a noose is you can use it more than once."

"There ain't no call to ponder nooses," Boyce said.

"The water's yet murky on all of this," Ansel agreed, "and it looks to be murky for a while yet."

"If you old men ain't got the stomach for it, head on back to town," Jubel said. "Right, Chauncey?"

The men turned to Chauncey, and it wasn't a bunch of boys waiting for orders but three men, two of them a good thirty years older and Boyce a Spanish War veteran.

"That's right," Chauncey said to Boyce and Ansel, "though after what the Huns did to your nephew I'd have thought you all to be the first to help."

Boyce and Ansel didn't respond but they didn't leave. In a few minutes two hounds came out of the woods with Linville stumbling behind, the leashes jerking and swaying in his hands.

"Left the wagon and other dogs at Slidell's," Linville said, "but these two are the proudest in the pack."

"This is his," Boyce said.

He handed the chambray shirt to Linville, who wadded it and let the dogs nuzzle the cloth before unleashing them. The hounds circled the yard until one gave a long moan and made a low-nosed rush into the woods, the other close behind.

"They've struck it," Linville said.

"Let Linville ride with you, Wilber," Chauncey said, and turned Traveler toward the far ridge.

At first the dogs and horses followed a discernible path through the woods. They came to a creek and for a few moments the hounds were confused. Then the dogs found the scent and followed it downstream. Chauncey and his horse splashed through the creek, then back onto the bank, weaving their way through woods and water. A branch knocked off Chauncey's hat but that no longer mattered. He didn't need a sign of rank to lead.

Jubel pulled close to Chauncey.

"That Hun's headed for the river."

Chauncey took the lead again and soon glimpsed water beyond the blur of trees. Suddenly, the woods ended and he was on a narrow riverbank with the hounds and Laurel Shelton. Chauncey pulled out the pistol as the rest of the search party floundered onto the swath of sand.

"Where's the Hun?" Chauncey shouted above the riders attempting to calm their mounts.

Laurel Shelton was backed against a tree, the hounds barking and slobbering as they surrounded her. Jack shouted that there was a shirt in the river. All the while, men and dogs and horses bumped and stumbled and circled. Traveler lost his footing for a moment and veered perilously close to the water. Chauncey had the dizzying sensation that he was on a horse astride a carousel, the world turning around him.

"Tether them damn dogs," Jubel shouted.

Linville dismounted and worked through the confusion of boots and hooves, lunging with the leash collar to snare the hounds and drag them away.

"Did he swim across the river?" Chauncey shouted, aiming the gun at Laurel, letting her and everyone else know he wasn't going to be trifled with, not today or ever again.

Laurel met his eyes and nodded just as a hound bumped Traveler's shanks and the horse jerked sideways.

Chauncey squeezed the rein to hold on and the pistol fired.

Traveler reared but Chauncey stayed in the saddle. Other horses whinnied and swerved and Jubel's mount almost tumbled into the river. The horses finally quieted and Linville pulled the dogs off the bank and into the woods. The world no longer spun around Chauncey. It had shuddered to a stop and locked itself into place. Laurel Shelton's back still pressed against the tree, but now a tear appeared in the green cloth covering her left breast. She didn't appear to be in pain, her face expressionless. It's a briar scratch, not a bullet hole, Chauncey told himself. Then her knees buckled and she fell to the ground.

For a few moments no one spoke. The men and boys watched as a stain spread down the dress. It was Boyce Clayton who moved first, kneeling beside her. He spoke her name. When there was no response, he took her wrist in his and searched for something not found.

"You killed a damn woman," Boyce said, turning to Chauncey.

Between sobs, Wilber said he wanted to go home.

"It was an accident," Chauncey said. "It wouldn't have happened if she hadn't been helping a spy."

"What the hell do you think he was spying on," Boyce asked, "down here in the middle of nowhere?"

"It was you all's fault," Chauncey said, "bumping and shoving. You should have kept your horses farther back. Those dogs too. They caused it to happen."

Boyce lifted Laurel Shelton into his arms. Ansel came over and stood beside him.

"You tell that to Hank," Boyce said. "He'll kill you for this."

"But it's Linville's fault more than mine," Chauncey said. "Those dogs should have been leashed the whole time."

"It ain't none of my fault," Linville said. "You shouldn't have had that damn pistol out, much less aiming it at her."

"I didn't aim it at her," Chauncey answered. "I aimed at the tree in case that Hun was hiding behind it. The dogs were what made it go off, and all of you bunching up on me."

"That Hun's getting away," Jubel said. "Let's go. The bridge ain't but a mile if we follow the river."

"I'm taking Laurel back to town," Boyce said. "I ain't leaving her out here."

"I ain't going either," Ansel said.

"I want to go back with you," Wilber whispered between sobs.

"Me too," Jack said.

Ansel helped Boyce drape the body on the horse.

"Quicker to follow the water," Boyce said and led them downriver, the only sound Wilber's sniffling.

The others didn't speak until the procession was out of sight.

"I got to get my wagon and the rest of my dogs," Linville said, "though if I hear another word about what's happened being my fault, I'll let you two sniff the ground and find that Hun."

Linville whistled and barks responded from above. He studied the steep terrain.

"Slidell's house can't be more than a quarter-mile up this ridge," Linville told them.

"It's too steep for the horses," Jubel said.

"But not me and these dogs," Linville replied. "You take the low road and we'll meet at the bridge."

As Linville and the dogs began their ascent, Jubel turned to Chauncey.

"You didn't do nothing that witch didn't deserve."

Chauncey nodded.

"We need to get on across that bridge," Jubel said. "It's already getting darksome and he ain't twiddling his thumbs waiting for us."

"You go on," Chauncey said. "I'm going back to find out from Shelton where that Hun's headed."

Jubel met his eyes for a long moment, then nodded.

"We'll meet across the river."

As Chauncey followed the creek upstream, he suddenly remembered Paul's homecoming. It would be over now, Senator Zeller and everybody else long gone, if it had even happened without Chauncey to supervise. He hadn't wanted to be here, but if he hadn't everyone in Mars Hill would have said Chauncey Feith was a coward, even though it wasn't his duty to lead a posse. Now there'd be people blaming him because he had left, just like they'd blame him for what was clearly an accident. If Jubel and the others hadn't come crowding in and the dogs hadn't been scaring the horses, it wouldn't have happened. Of course Jubel was right. The real blame was with the Shelton bitch. If she hadn't been helping a damn Hun escape, Chauncey wouldn't have had his pistol out in the first place. As soon as she saw him, she should have lain down on the ground because, for all Chauncey knew, that Hun was behind the tree with his own gun. If she'd been on the ground with her hands out, the bullet would have just hit the tree.

Chauncey came to where the creek and the trail to the cabin met. Because he was riding slower and alone, he noticed how quiet the woods were. Too quiet. No birds sang or squirrels chattered, the only sound the leaves under Traveler's feet, soft and breathy like someone, or something, whispering. He passed more dead chestnuts than he'd ever seen in one place and even the oaks and the poplars had few leaves, their gray bony branches piercing the sky. After a while, he passed graves he hadn't noticed earlier, two graves. Chauncey had the chilling thought that this cove already knew what he was going to do.

He was still in the woods when he dismounted and leashed Traveler to a dogwood sapling. When he came out of the trees, he was directly in front of the porch. Hank was still tied up. Since he'd helped harbor a Hun, Hank would get put in jail, but even so one day he'd surely be let out. Chauncey had no choice, because that was what war was—killing a man so he wouldn't kill you. You can't give him a chance because he can't give you one and every soldier understood that.

I'll not shoot him in the back though, Chauncey told himself, and it isn't only to show he was attacking me. I'll kill him like a man. He moved across the yard and stood in front of the steps. Hank had his chin tucked against his chest and knees. His eyes were closed as if he was asleep, but then Chauncey saw the shoulders shrugging to free the arm. Chauncey looked to his right, on past the scaffold to check the path they'd followed into the cove, then left beyond the railing where Hank was tied, and saw no one there either. He took the pistol from his holster and settled his index finger inside the curve of the metal, not touching the trigger. The gun felt five times as heavy as before and Chauncey was suddenly engulfed in weariness.

It was so unfair. If he'd just been allowed to stay at the homecoming ceremony, none of this would have happened. The damn Claytons had to pick this day, after who knew how long, to figure out they'd been playing music and having a high old time with a spy, then expect Chauncey to come into this godforsaken place and track the Hun down when they should have done it by themselves. Now he was going to have to do this. No one would give him a medal or say he was a hero the way they would if Chauncey did the exact same thing in France or Belgium. There would be people in Mars Hill who wouldn't believe Hank Shelton had attacked him or even tried to run away. They'd think Chauncey shot Hank when he was still tied to the porch railing. Because that was what they wanted to believe, that Chauncey Feith couldn't have done it any other way, and it'd be the very same folks who just hours ago slapped him on the back and tipped their hats and told him what a bully fellow he was. The very same ones.

The hell with them, Chauncey thought, and with the Claytons and the Sheltons and that German professor and that hag librarian and Meachum and Estep and that damn escaped Hun too. They could every one of them go straight to hell for all Chauncey cared. There was nothing he could do to please any of them so they could think what they wanted. Chauncey let the crook of his index finger touch the trigger. All he had to do was squeeze it. Just walk up there and do it and do it now and you won't be down here when it's full dark. He thought of the bottles hung on the tree limb. A witch, that was what people, a lot of people, believed Laurel Shelton was. The same folks would also believe that a witch could seed a place with all sorts of charms and hexes that could still live on even if the witch didn't.

Chauncey stepped onto the porch and pointed the pistol at Hank's chest. It wasn't until the third shot that he heard the solid thunk of the bullet finding its mark. He fired the magazine's last three bullets and twice more heard metal hit flesh. Chauncey opened his eyes. The acrid odor of cordite filled the porch. Chauncey let himself look at one board in front of him and then another and then one more until he saw the soles of Hank's boots. He let his eyes rise a little more and saw the pants and then the darkening shirttail. All the while, like Laurel, there hadn't been a cry or moan, just silence. You've got to be sure, Chauncey told himself, and raised his eyes higher and saw the first bullet hole in the upper stomach and the second in the middle of the chest. You don't have to look for the third one. Just go untie him and drag him off the porch and leave. But he couldn't stop himself. His eyes lifted and he saw where the third bullet had entered Hank's cheek. Hank stared straight at Chauncey, the manner of his gaze not accusing or angry or even sad. It was something worse. What light Hank's eyes held faded, not dying away like an ember but receding like a train headed elsewhere. Chauncey couldn't shake the feeling that wherever the light was going it was taking part of him with it.

Chauncey stepped off the porch and went to the side railing to untie Hank. The knot was tight and his fingers shook so bad he couldn't free the rope. He tried using his forefinger and thumb but a nail snagged in the hemp and broke off. The finger started bleeding and it was just one more thing gone wrong. Chauncey went inside the cabin and found a butcher knife. He was about to cut the rope when a horse snorted.

Through the railing he saw Slidell Hampton coming out

of the woods. Just hide in the shadows and see what he does, Chauncey decided. To take the body back to town, he'll have to unknot the rope. Then it's Hampton's word against yours that Shelton was shot while tied up. Who should any fair-minded person believe, Chauncey told himself, an old codger who's known for months the Sheltons were hiding a Hun, or a man who wears the uniform. Yet there'd be folks who'd expect Chauncey to prove what he claimed, as if a soldier needed to justify killing an American in league with a Hun spy. It was treason and the army shot men for that and shot them with their hands tied behind their backs, but some people in town would still get all righteous about it. They'd expect Chauncey to prove he'd been nearly killed before he shot Hank Shelton, proof like a bullet in his leg or arm. Or a knife cut.

By god he'd give it to them then, Chauncey vowed as he stepped back from the porch. He'd show them the butcher knife and a wound, then dare them to their faces to say they'd have done different. He'd make the cut on his forearm, like he'd been fending Shelton off. That would shut them up. There might even be a medal after all. He could do it right now, just take the knife and rake it across his forearm. It looked sharp enough to go right through the shirt cloth and into the skin. But it would hurt.

No, he'd do it later, Chauncey decided as Slidell dismounted. I'll do it when I can see and cut careful so the knife won't go deep, only enough to draw blood. Chauncey took another step back and shadows almost fully enveloped him. If he hasn't seen me yet, he's not going to see me now, Chauncey told himself. Just stay out of sight until he leaves. Chauncey lifted his foot to take a final step back and the ground was not there and he was falling into the darkest place he had ever known.

CHAPTER TWENTY-FIVE

Walter stayed at the outcrop until dusk. Laurel's quilt was where she had laid it, and he left it there, made his way up to the campsite. Come full dark, he tucked himself knees to chest in a burrow of leaves. Dawn finally came and he waited. Twice the woods stirred, soft footfalls coming nearer, but each time it was a deer, once a fawn, then a buck whose branching antlers were such a wonder that he first thought it an hallucination. That evening he went down the opposite slope and found a few shriveled apples.

On the third morning, Walter woke to a gunshot, then a second and a third. He walked up to the ridge crest and saw the farmer in his yard, shotgun in hand. The boom of shotguns and crackle of rifles came from farther away, then even farther, the blasts like firecrackers set rattling down the valley. The farmer raised his gun skyward and pulled the trigger a last time, unbuckled the stock from the barrel, and removed the spent shell.

What the gunshots meant, Walter did not know, but he turned and started down the ridge. He looked through the trees for chimney smoke. What he saw made him break into a run. It's just livestock they killed, he told himself, but as the woods thinned he saw the buzzards gliding above the cabin. He tripped and twisted his ankle, got up and went on. As he came into the yard a buzzard, wings spread, hopped off the porch, balancing itself briefly on two scabby yellow legs before taking flight.

There were no bodies on the porch, just what looked like a spill of tar. No one was inside the cabin either. He went out in the yard and shouted Laurel's name and it echoed off the cliff and ridge, then silence. He called again and again until his voice was no more than a rasp. An hour passed before he left the porch and took the path up to the notch. Slidell was not in the house. As Walter stepped off the porch, he saw the two mounds of fresh dirt.

After a few minutes, he walked on toward Mars Hill. Walter was almost to the main road when he heard dogs barking. He thought the men were on their way back so stopped and waited, glad he wouldn't have to walk any farther to have it over with. But the dogs' barks grew distant. He was lightheaded from the lack of food and his body too felt lighter, unfleshed, only the weight of bone left to carry it forward. Walter went on. He passed cabins and then houses in which no one appeared to be home. Before long he heard music and then shouts amid spurts of fireworks, gunshots. The road rose a last time and he saw the town was filled with revelers. Small flags waved from children's fists and adults cheered and shouted. Red, white, and blue streamers hung from storefronts and musicians played. A man raised a pistol and fired at the sky while two couples danced a reel. Four men walked past with linked arms as they drunkenly sang. Walter looked for familiar faces but saw none, and no one took notice of him though he walked down the middle of the street. Slidell's wagon was tethered beside the saloon. A barkeep exited the swinging doors with a brass spittoon and poured out tobacco juice. Walter followed the barkeep inside.

After the expansive midday light, the room was at first only darkness. Men had been talking but, as Walter's sight adjusted, the sound, as if in some necessary balancing, lessened. Glasses and bottles emerged above the muted shine of the bar, then the barkeep's face and the backs of the two drinkers, last the wide mirror's reflections. One of the men was the red-bearded man who had been at the cabin, beside him another much older man. Both stared into their shot glasses. The bartender held his rag steady on the counter as though staunching a leak.

"You wanted me, so I am here," Walter said.

Silver coins spilled onto the bar, their ringing against the varnished wood slapped mute by the red-haired man's broad hand. He muttered something and turned from the bar, as did the man beside him. Walter waited for them to come at him but they instead stepped around and out the saloon doors.

"So you can talk. I've been wondering about that for months now."

Walter turned and saw Slidell in the corner. On his table was a half-empty bottle of whiskey. Slidell's eyes were bloodshot, his clothes rumpled and dirty as Walter's. He motioned toward the swinging doors.

"The war may be over, but it's not smart baiting fellows like you just did."

"The graves," Walter asked. "They are Laurel's and Hank's, aren't they?"

"Yes," Slidell answered. "I wasn't sure where to bury Hank, but I'd made a promise to Laurel. It seemed they ought to be together."

"They were killed because they helped me?"

"I don't know," Slidell answered. "Some who were there claim Chauncey Feith didn't mean to shoot Laurel, but him shooting Hank was no accident."

Slidell nodded toward the saloon doors.

"I think you better leave here, and I mean out of the whole town. That son of a bitch Wray may be coming back."

"The man who killed Hank and Laurel, where is he?"

"I don't know and nobody else seems to know either," Slidell said, glancing at the entrance. "Feith's horse wandered into town two days ago, but that could just have been a ploy. Most folks figure his daddy sneaked him onto the train, or he sneaked on himself. That way he can stay clear of here until things settle a while, then come back. Or maybe not come back. He'd not be the first to do that. But no one saw him get on the train, or at least admits it. Feith could still be in the cove. Folks have been known to disappear down there."

Slidell lifted his glass and drank what was left, stood and looked at Meachum.

"How long till the next passenger train?"

Meachum checked the clock above the mirror.

"Twenty minutes if it's on time."

Slidell came around the table and stood beside Walter.

"You need to be on that train."

"I have no money with me," Walter said.

"Your fife and other belongings there too?" Slidell asked.

Walter nodded.

Slidell opened a leather wallet and took out all but one bill.

"Here," he said, and stuffed the money in Walter's shirt pocket. "That's enough to get you to New York. Write me when you get there and I'll send your belongings. Come on, we'll get your ticket and wait on the platform."

Walter didn't move.

"You knew I was German all along?"

"Not until I brought you to town that morning," Slidell answered. "I went to the depot to make sure you'd gotten on the train okay. The depot master said he hadn't seen you. There was a wanted poster in there with a sketch of you on it."

"Why didn't you tell?"

"That morning, it was because bastards like Feith and Jubel Parton wouldn't wait for the law. If they knew, they'd hunt you down and kill you. You hadn't hurt Laurel or Hank and I knew you weren't a spy or a soldier. But later . . ."

Slidell looked at the floor. He pressed the bridge of his nose with a thumb and finger, looked up, and met Walter's gaze.

"But later," Slidell said, "because you were the one chance for Laurel to have some happiness in her life. And she did, for a little while."

For a few moments, Slidell looked like he might say more, but he didn't. He took Walter by the arm and led him through the doors. They stepped onto the boardwalk just as the redheaded man and a companion came toward them, axe handles and rope in their hands. The one who led gestured with an axe handle.

"Get back in there, Hun."

"The war's over, Jubel," Slidell said.

"Not until we find out what he done to Chauncey," Jubel said. "Then this town's going to have use for that grandstand after all."

Jubel poked the handle into Walter's chest, pushed him back inside.

"Go on home, old man," the red-headed man said, and left Slidell on the boardwalk.

"Pull down your shutters and bolt the real doors, Meachum," Jubel ordered. "We're having us a private party tonight."

Meachum had just pulled the shutters down when Slidell came in, a raised double-barreled shotgun in his hands.

"If you don't think I'll use it, you better mull this over," Slidell said. "I've already lived four days longer than I wish I had. Hank and Laurel, they were the last thing I cared about on this earth. What happened to them, you had your part in it."

Slidell turned to Walter.

"Get on that train. If need be, you can switch to one headed to New York at the next depot. Go, go now."

Walter walked out into the afternoon's brightness. A banner hung from the savings and loan's awning, one word on it, VICTORY. As he walked over to the depot, Walter stepped around a limp string of firecrackers, small flags, and a brass-capped shotgun shell. Inside the train station, the wanted poster was no longer on the wall. The depot master gave him his ticket and told him the train left in twelve minutes. He went outside and sat on a bench, watched the clock tower's minute hand make ten measured lurches before the train arrived. The conductor set down a wooden footstool, nodded for Walter and the two other passengers to board. He found an empty window seat but did not look out through the glass until the wheels began to turn. He stared at the mountains and thought how small and fleeting a human life was. Forty or fifty years, a blink of time for these mountains, and there'd be no memory of what had happened here.

He leaned his head into his palms and closed his eyes, did not open them until a voice asked for his ticket. Walter handed the conductor the ticket and turned to the window, watched the world rush past him.

The train had rumbled into Maryland before his head cleared enough to remember why he was returning to New York. It was harder to remember why it once had been so important to him. He tried to imagine some alternative, another place, another profession, but could not. New York, then. After Slidell sent the flute, he would go to Goritz and tell the conductor that what had been asked of Walter was now done. He would tell Goritz that he was ready.